EVOLVED

THE IMMORTAL ONES - BOOK TWO

Shade Owens

EVOLVED – THE IMMORTAL ONES, BOOK TWO
© Copyright 2021 Shade Owens
www.shadeowens.com

SERIES INFORMATION

Chosen - Book One
Evolved – Book Two
Hunted – Book Three
Ignited – Book Four
Risen – Book Five

Edited by Nikki Busch
www.nikkibuschediting.com

Published by

RED RAVEN PUBLISHING

ISBN: 978-1-990271-88-5

CHAPTER 1

There was so much blood.

At first, I wondered if maybe I'd gone back in time to the day Grandma let me paint on my wall with beet juice. Was this beet juice? I'd never seen so much red before.

Star lay lifeless, her blond hair sticking to her clammy neck. She looked paler than her usual ghost-white complexion. I glanced up at the nearest cliff, imagining how painful her fall from the railroad must have been. Had they thrown her out carelessly as they'd done to me? Had they not cared that she'd been stitched up after pregnancy?

Probably not.

I wanted to feel sorry for her—sad at the idea that if she managed to survive this, she would wake up with a slit in her belly and no baby in her arms. But I was too shocked by the blood to feel anything other than horror. How could they have done this to her? They'd torn her child right out of her and sewn her up poorly like they *wanted* her stitches to tear open.

"This isn't good," Penelope said. She searched furiously through a pouch around her waist. She unclipped it, the blood on her hands soaking through the light beige material, then reached inside. "If we don't control the bleeding, she'll die. She's already lost too much blood."

Penelope looked like she knew what she was doing. Was she a doctor? A nurse? She stared intently at Star's wound, her chocolate-brown eyes narrowing as she no doubt played countless scenarios in her mind. Although she wore many layers of animal hide and green, leaflike clothes, which added to her bulk, her frame looked small. Her jaw was slim and defined, and her neck was slender. A tiny nose with uneven nostrils sat in the middle of her face, and as she concentrated on helping Star, several creases formed between her straight eyebrows.

"This'll work," she said, peering inside her small bag.

Her hair, a chestnut brown, hung braided behind her back. It was a unique style I'd never seen before; it started up high on her head, keeping her hair out of her face, and ran down to the ends of her hair. The people of Lutum typically had simple hair styles—either loose or tied up and usually unkempt.

As I admired her big braid, I noticed that part of her left ear was missing. At the top, a chunk had either been cut off, or bitten off by some wild animal. I didn't ask. Maybe one day, she'd tell me about it. If we survived long enough.

I stared at Star's belly, which looked like it had been torn open by a monster. Blood poured out from one corner, while the rest of her skin remained loosely sewn together. A few remaining black threads stretched as her gash expanded. If we didn't act fast, the few remaining stitches would snap.

Penelope handed me a rag. "Keep this on there."

The cloth looked dirty, but I supposed this was the least of our worries. We either controlled the bleeding, or she died.

I grabbed the cloth and pressed it hard against Star's bare, pudgy belly. Blood pooled around the cloth, while most of it soaked into it, warming my fingertips. I wanted to pull away when I felt the wetness but reminded myself that the pressure I applied could very well be what kept her alive.

Penelope reached into her pouch again and extracted what appeared to be a needle and some thread.

My eyes bulged. "You're going to stitch her back up?"

Without a word, Penelope glanced up at me. It was a silent exchange that told me we had no other choice. Thankfully, Star was out cold, so she wouldn't feel the pain.

"You ready?" Penelope asked.

She extracted a glass bottle and went on to pour some clear liquid over Star's belly, causing a mass of pink to spread across Star's skin. Whatever this fluid was, it removed some of the gunk that had attached itself to the edges of the incision and seemed to clean away surface scum. Next, she poured that same liquid over her long needle, emptying the bottle.

I wasn't sure what it was, but I knew what she was doing—disinfecting what she could.

She flattened her lips into a narrow line, then held the needle in the air, its bottom end fastened to a piece of black thread.

I wasn't ready, but we had no other choice.

"You don't have to watch," she said.

I didn't say anything.

"Here." She handed me another cloth. "If she wakes up, put this in her mouth."

I wanted to ask her why, but there was no time. She drew in closer and I pulled the blood-soaked cloth away. It was heavy and smelled of iron.

Without hesitating, Penelope pressed the needle's sharp tip into Star's skin and began sewing her together. As she pulled hard, blood slipped through the open gash, and Star's belly jiggled. Sickening nausea filled my stomach, and though I wanted to look away, I couldn't bring myself to do it. Curious and eager to learn, I wanted to see skin being stitched together for the first time, despite how much it grossed me out.

Penelope pressed hard every time she drove the needle through Star's skin, and it made me weak in the knees. About halfway through the process, Star let out a bellow that made me jump back several feet. Her eyes opened wide like she was seeing a ghost, and she searched the sky for something or someone. She kicked the air and swung a hand upward as if trying to catch a cloud.

"Star, it's me," Penelope said. "Stay calm. We're trying to help you."

She jerked her chin at me, ordering me to stick the cloth in Star's mouth.

I did as instructed, causing Star to gag a few times. But she didn't fight me. Instead, she stared straight up, not once blinking.

"Hey," I whispered. "It's okay. Penelope's almost done."

Her body stopped twitching and Penelope finished sewing her up. Did she not feel the pain? Why wasn't she moving anymore? She stared at the sky without blinking.

"Star?" I asked.

Nothing.

"Star?"

Something was wrong.

Penelope dropped her needle and sighed.

Star's eyes seemed to glaze over with a milky substance. I wanted to reach for her face or shake her until she blinked, but it was pointless. She was already gone.

Penelope dropped back into a seated position, her face in her palms. Blood spread across her cheeks and forehead, but she didn't seem to care.

With her lower lip trembling, she crawled up to Star's face, kissed her forehead, and closed her eyes with the tips of her fingers. "You will be avenged, my friend."

CHAPTER 2

Penelope marched through the vast open field, her heavy attire chafing as she moved. I had to jog to keep up, but I didn't complain about it. I could tell she was hurting. She'd just lost one of her dearest friends.

How well had they known each other? Star had spoken about Penelope inside Olympus and how she'd been the last one to leave them. Being that Star had seniority when I arrived, this meant that the two of them had spent several years at each other's sides.

"We need to keep searching," Penelope said.

"For the others?" I asked.

Rather than respond, she led me back into the same forest where I'd nearly been eaten by wolves.

"We need to follow the tracks," she said.

By tracks, she meant the railroad tracks up

above. Although I couldn't see them, I knew they followed the edge of the cliff. We hadn't ventured far into the forest when she led me to a large tree with some missing bark. It was the biggest tree in sight, and from one of its crooked branches hung a horn of sorts. It dangled from a worn rope, swaying slightly. She grabbed it, untied it, then placed it to her lips. When she blew hard, her cheeks ballooned. Out from the other end came a bellowing sound that made me turn my head away. It was deep, far-reaching, and even musical.

"What's that?" I asked when she tied it back up.

"A signal," she said.

She didn't look at me. Instead, she glared in the distance, her focus narrowing toward the mountains. Was she waiting for something to happen? For someone to appear?

Soon, the sound of galloping echoed nearby.

It was difficult to see much through the trees. But every few seconds, I caught a glimpse of the approaching stranger—a woman on a black-and-white horse. From this distance, she was small and fuzzy, but the closer she got, the more detail I could make out. Next to her was another horse with a saddle but no rider. It followed her like an obedient dog, trotting at her side.

They strode through the open field, entered the forest, and arrived next to us.

The woman was dressed similarly to Penelope, in layers of fur and leaflike fabric. Around her waist was a belt holding several knives, ropes, and other gadgets I couldn't quite make out. Her boots, thick and leathery, made me think of soldiers from the ancient wars Grandma often spoke about.

"Greer, this is Silver, one of the survivors," Penelope said without looking at me.

Greer tried to smile, but it looked like more of a twitch of the lip. Her face, aged and worn, reminded me of what the Elites feared most. Around her eyes were countless lines and wrinkles. When she tried to smile, her lips pulled downward involuntarily like she'd spent the last decade frowning. Yet a sweetness lingered behind those gray eyes—something that told me I was in good hands. She wasn't as old as Grandma, but her short salt-and-pepper hair gave her age away. Her cheekbones, two little hills under her eyes, complemented her square head and wide jaw.

"Come," she said, extending a strong-looking hand down to me.

Come where? What did she mean by this?

Penelope pressed a gentle hand on my shoulder. "Greer will bring you to Ortus, our village."

"Village?" I mumbled.

Greer shook her hand in the air, urging me to grab on. Reluctantly, I moved forward and grabbed her hand. She clutched my wrist firmly and said, "Place your foot right there and pull yourself up."

I did as she'd told me, nearly falling back as I tried to climb onto the horse behind her and into what looked to be a second seat. Thankfully, Penelope caught me and pushed me up.

Without any effort, Penelope climbed onto the other horse. "You'll be okay. Hang on, do as you're told, and I'll do my best to find your friends."

I parted my lips to thank her, but she kicked the sides of her horse and cried out, "Hiya!"

Within seconds, Penelope disappeared through the trees.

"Don't be afraid," Greer said. "Hold on to my waist."

I felt awkward holding on to a stranger, but I did so anyway. I'd never been on a horse before. It was exciting and terrifying all at the same time. She did the same as Penelope had done—squeezing her legs around the horse's torso—and off we went.

My heart skipped a beat as the horse galloped and I bounced up and down.

It hurt my butt, but even more, my injured ribs.

Every time I came down on the saddle, I cringed, wanting the ride to be over.

"How far away is this village?" I asked through clenched teeth.

Greer gently tugged at the reins and the horse slowed down. "Are you injured?"

I nodded, but when I realized she couldn't see me, I said, "Yeah, a bit."

"We'll take it slow," she said. "Ortus is about an hour from here depending on how fast you're traveling."

I imagined that meant it would take longer if the horse wasn't running. Not that I minded. I wasn't sure how much more bouncing I could handle.

Greer led the horse across an open field and toward another forest. I must have held on tighter to her waist as we entered. She turned her head slightly to the side. "I know you're scared, but you're safe up here, okay?"

I nodded again, forgetting she couldn't see me.

Every time something cracked nearby, or leaves rustled, my heartbeat doubled and I snapped my head sideways, trying to locate the source of the sound. Were there wolves in this forest, too? Or worse, bears? I'd never seen a bear in real life before, but after seeing how big wolves were, I was afraid to come face-to-face with a bear. I never imagined wolves could be so big, so terrifying.

After a while, I realized that this forest was filled mostly with red foxes—something I wished I'd one day get to see—and squirrels of all colors. We didn't get much wildlife in Lutum and it was something I cherished.

I gazed in awe as a slender red fox approached a rotting log and sniffed its insides. What was it looking for? Food? I smiled at the creature, breathing in the forest's fresh scent of pine and moist earth.

"This is Death Valley," came Greer's voice.

With my attention now pulled away from the fox, I searched the road ahead of us. Greer's attire was so heavy and layered, the brown fur tickled the underneath of my chin as I peered over her shoulder. As we exited the forest, we stepped onto a dirt path that seemed to never end. It led far away and in between two massive mountains. I craned my neck, excited at the thought of having reached the ominous mountains I'd seen earlier through the train windows.

Greer turned her head sideways, a crooked smile pulling at her weathered face. "First mountain, huh?"

I stared wide-eyed, too shocked to say anything. The closer we got to entering Death

Valley, the more excited I became. The mountains seemed to grow taller and taller the closer we got.

I wanted to ask why they called something so magnificent *Death Valley*, but its name was obvious—everything looked dead. It was almost as if a wall of fire had swept between the mountains, destroying everything in its wake.

"As you can see, nothing grows here," Greer said. She pointed at the mountainsides. "They block too much of the sun."

The path wasn't narrow by any means—at least fifty yards wide—but I suspected that Death Valley only got an hour or two of sunlight each day, right around the afternoon mark. Having been raised in Division 9—the division of agriculture—I understood the importance of sunlight.

I sat quietly, listening to the horse's hooves against the hard surface.

"This path leads to Ortus," Greer said without looking back.

"Aren't you ever afraid the Elites will come looking for you?"

She shifted in her saddle and smirked back at me. "The Elites believe in superstition and myths. They also believe the tale we fabricated about Death Valley, and how anyone who dares roam this area will be met with instant death, forced to live an eternal life of torment and bone-crushing torture."

I got chills at the thought of it but quickly reminded myself that it was only a story intended to arouse fear.

It worked.

"Who came up with that?" I asked.

"Finn," she said. "You'll meet him soon."

"He's also the one who—" she began but froze midsentence.

At once, she tugged on the reins of her horse and the creature stopped walking.

She started speaking again. "Do you hear—"

At once, the horse neighed furiously and reared onto its back legs, throwing me off the saddle. I was too confused by what was happening to even try to hold on to Greer. Instead, I slipped backward, landing awkwardly on one foot and one knee. Greer shot a glance at me, but she didn't have time to say or do anything. Without warning, the horse landed back on all fours and took off into Death Valley with Greer yanking wildly on its reins, trying to regain control.

I sat still in the crumbly dirt, trying to understand what had happened. Though I considered chasing after Greer and the horse, something told me the horse got spooked for a reason. I searched the trees in the distance behind me, afraid of what I might find.

But there was nothing.

A faint hissing sound caught my attention. It came from above, growing louder and more distinct as it moved.

What was that?

I squinted up at the clouds, trying to locate the source of the sound.

And then, I found it. Although I didn't know what it was, I got the feeling it wasn't good. The gadget, a small, white, circular-shaped thing, flew in oval motions, its shiny black front rolling in every direction like an eyeball.

What was that thing? A camera? I'd never seen one in real life.

I jumped up and ran to the edge of the mountain where a crevasse sank into the stone and pressed my back against the solid wall. Overhead, a protruding rock shadowed me, hiding me from whatever that gadget was.

The strange contraption flew around for a few more minutes as if searching for something. When it either found what it wanted or didn't find anything, it shot upright into the clouds and disappeared.

I stood quietly, holding on to my aching ribs as the sun rose above Death Valley. It cast a yellow hue across the lifeless path, illuminating crisp branches, pebbles of all shapes and sizes, and a few insects that scurried across the dry, sandy path.

Would Greer be waiting for me at the end of the valley? And if so, how long was the trek? My mind raced as I contemplated my different options. If I walked, I risked running into threats I knew nothing about, including people who might view me as an enemy. But if I remained here, I exposed myself to wild animals or more of those floating camera devices.

If it had spooked the horse, it meant it wasn't a standard occurrence. That also led me to believe that whoever was controlling that floating machine wasn't on our side.

I closed my eyes as the heat of the sun warmed the tips of my toes. Maybe if I remained close to the mountain, I would be safe. I craned my neck, appreciating the overhead canopy I'd managed to hide under.

Sighing, I lowered myself into a seated position and waited.

Greer would come back for me.

Right?

CHAPTER 3

When the sound of galloping approached, I poked my head out from behind the cliff canopy. In the distance came Greer, leaning forward on her horse as she soared through Death Valley.

When she reached me, she commanded her horse to stop and its hooves slid through the dirt.

"Silver, I'm so sorry," she said, out of breath. "Are you all right?"

"I'm okay," I said.

She offered me a hand and this time, I didn't hesitate and immediately pulled myself up onto the horse.

"What was that?" I asked.

"Something we don't usually see here," she said.

Without another word, she kicked the sides of her horse and we took off galloping faster than I was prepared for. I held on tight as the wind swept through my hair and slipped past my lips, drying my throat. The sun had already begun to disappear overhead, descending behind the mountain. A cool shadow loomed over us as we strode between the mountains and I breathed in the clean air.

Unlike Lutum, the air around here felt light and clean. It wasn't like Lutum was polluted, or anything, but the energy surrounding Lutum felt heavy, dark, and hopeless.

Out here, it felt like anything was possible— like maybe if I closed my eyes and wished hard enough, I might be able to fly. I knew the thought was silly, but maybe this was what freedom felt like.

We made our way around a bend as the horse's hooves clacked against the crushed rock. But rather than continue down the bend, Greer made the horse slow down. With the reins, she pulled its head sideways and led us toward what appeared to be a stone wall.

Where was she taking us? Was she turning around?

She patted her horse on the neck to praise it, then descended, her boot swiftly grazing the top of my head. I was thankful for her flexibility.

"Wait here," she ordered.

I sat on the horse, nervous. What if it took off again? What if something spooked it?

Awkward, I patted the side of its round belly, hoping to soothe the creature. It was warm and so big that I felt like a young child.

Greer moved toward a large black boulder that appeared smooth and lustrous, almost as if it didn't belong to the rest of the mountain. She knelt next to it and tossed a pebble under a narrow crack.

What the heck was she doing?

Two beige pebbles came rolling out from behind the boulder. She picked these up, examined them, and rolled only one of them back into the crack.

Unexpectedly, the boulder shifted.

I widened my eyes as the rock rolled sideways, revealing two tall men dressed in the same attire as Greer—beige hemp, fur shoulder pads, and all sorts of straps and weapons fastened around their waists. They looked primitive as if they'd been born and raised away from civilization. The man on the left—the taller of the two with dark brown skin, a robust black beard, and curly hair to match—greeted Greer by clasping wrists with her. It was like a handshake, only higher up on the arm. He patted her firmly on the back, then shifted his gaze to me.

"A survivor?" His voice was deep and grainy.

Greer nodded. "We lost one. Penelope went searching for the others. Silver says four more women were thrown from the train."

The bearded man searched his boots, clearly saddened by the news. "I'm sorry."

But the sad look on his face didn't last long.

"We have a problem, Jayun," Greer said.

Jayun's dark forehead wrinkled and he stepped closer to Greer. The second man—a brown-haired fellow with a smaller frame, sunken eyes, and a short, reddish beard—didn't seem as involved in the conversation. He appeared more concerned about Death Valley, likely wanting to ensure that no one had followed us. He held on to what appeared to be a bow and rested an arrow against the bowstring, prepared to fire at a moment's notice.

"The Eye came over Death Valley," Greer said.

Jayun pulled his face so far back that his beard folded at his neckline. "What? How is that possible? It never comes near Death Valley."

Greer shook her salt-and-pepper head, her short hair barely moving. "I don't know, but this is serious. We need to inform Finn."

What were they talking about? What was this Eye they spoke of? Was Greer referring to that object I saw flying in the sky? Did it belong to the Elites?

"I need to go back to Penelope," Greer said.

"Can you please take Silver to meet Finn?"

Jayun's eyes rolled up toward me and he smiled. "So, you're Silver."

I didn't know how to respond, so I didn't. Instead, I sat quietly on the horse, waiting for Greer to tell me to get down.

She moved toward me and stuck out a hand. "Come."

I held on tight and climbed off the horse, clutching the saddle for dear life as I slid down.

"You're okay," she said, helping me reach the ground.

I stumbled and landed in her arms.

"Jayun will bring you to Finn," she said. "I promise you'll be in good hands."

Jayun smiled again, while the man next to him searched the sky with a scowl on his face.

Jayun didn't have to say anything for me to know he wanted me to follow him. I walked past Greer and entered the strange opening. The air was cool and damp, and around us were walls made of stone. What was this place? A cavern? Was their village hidden inside a mountain?

Jayun reached for a torch and pulled it out of its sconce, an orange glow spreading several yards away from us. The other man didn't follow. Instead, he stood at the entrance and with a large wooden stick, rolled the boulder back into position. It locked into place, making a crunching sound, and darkened the tunnel even more.

Jayun looked down at me and it hurt my neck to look up at him. The man was very tall—taller than any man I'd ever met before. He raised his torch toward the purple, crystallized ceiling and said, "This here leads the way to our village, Ortus."

"I heard about it," I said.

The sound of pebbles rolling echoed as we walked through the dimly lit tunnel. It was an eerie, hollow sound, and I didn't like it.

He smiled again, his beard expanding around his mouth. "You don't have to be afraid. It's a bit dark, but do you see that light over there?" He pointed toward the end of the cavern and I nodded. "That's the entrance to our village. It isn't far." He aimed his eyes at my ribs, and only then did I realize I was still holding on to them. "Are you okay to walk?"

I nodded, wondering how he might have responded if I'd said no. Would he have carried me? I looked at his arms, one of which was easily the size of both my legs combined, if not larger. This man was huge. Maybe that was why he was responsible for guarding the main entrance.

He led the way down the tunnel and I followed, wondering if bats were sleeping overhead. Would my friends come through here, too? Were they even alive? I thought of Danika, Dax, Asako, Rose, and Echo. I missed them. Despite having only spent a few days getting to know these women, I felt as though we'd grown close.

I hoped they were okay.

When we reached the end of the cavern, Jayun placed his torch into an empty sconce on the wall. I stepped out onto a flat rock platform, my eyes narrowing at the bright sun shining down on me.

The village was busy, crowded, and full of life, but my attention was immediately drawn to the village's perimeter. All around us, mountains stood tall, forming a circle-like enclosure around the village. The mountains were so high that I had to crane my neck to look at their peaks. Tall grass and trees sat decoratively around their bases and traveled up near the tops, where gray stone and fresh white snow reached for the sky.

Countless voices bounced around through the village, drawing my attention back to where people of all different heights and ethnicities walked, tending to daily chores. Two thin women with light brown skin hung clothes to dry, while one man sitting in a wooden wheelchair rolled down a dirt path, laughing and chasing after children who were kicking a ball.

Homes constructed of wood with hay roofs took up a good portion of the village, but farther down was an open field filled with young adults fighting with sticks and wooden swords. A large wooden fence wrapped around the field, blocking most of the fighters from view. But now and then, someone swooped out, swinging a wooden sword at their opponent.

It made loud clacking sounds that made me thankful I wasn't their enemy.

Near the cavern entrance was a beautiful lilac tree that hung low. As a gentle breeze swept by, some of its purple flower petals detached and floated toward the trim grass.

Around several homes were colorful gardens chock-full of pinks, purples, and yellows. People tended to the gardens, watering them with metallic watering cans much like the ones we were given in Lutum, only less damaged and far shinier.

Did vegetables grow there? Or were the gardens planted for beauty? I stared in awe, admiring the smooth, colorful petals, the thick green leaves, and the long stems.

"Some people like to garden," Jayun said, leaning into me.

"Some people?" I asked. "Do you mean they get to decide what to plant?"

He smiled but didn't answer.

"Over there are the garden beds." He pointed beyond the homes and near the open field where dozens upon dozens of raised garden beds lay side by side. Through the rows were adults working at plucking away weeds, and every few seconds, someone would laugh and point at something.

It was astonishing to see so many people smiling.

Lutum wasn't like this at all.

On the outskirts of the village were larger edifices constructed of wood, much like the individual homes, only bigger and more square-shaped. What were these used for? Education? I hoped they had a school here. I'd read so much about children going to school in the old days and always hoped that one day, I would be able to attend some type of school.

On the east side of the village, near the mountain wall, was a large building with a massive staircase leading up to a wraparound balcony. Everything was made of yellow wood and looked solid despite sitting high up in the air, supported by wooden poles all around. At the bottom of the staircase stood two armed men, both of them holding spears next to them.

I pointed at the building. "What's that?"

"That's where we're going," Jayun said. "Come."

CHAPTER 4

As we walked through the village, countless heads turned our way. Some eyes were wide and excited, while others were narrow and hostile. I couldn't understand how there could be such opposing reactions to my being here, but I figured it was best to wait until we were inside the building before I started asking Jayun a bunch of questions.

He led me to the two guards at the front of the staircase. They wore beige uniforms with padded shoulders and pockets over their chests. I considered saying hello to be polite, but neither of them looked at me, so I followed Jayun quietly. When he made a hand gesture, they turned sideways and made way, planting their spears firmly in the lush green grass next to their feet.

The wooden staircase creaked as we ascended, more so when Jayun took a step with his heavy boots. I tiptoed behind him, grazing the soft wooden railing as we moved closer and closer toward uncertainty. I stared at the wraparound balcony, wondering if it went all the way to the back of the building. It was such a unique structure that I couldn't help but smile.

Jayun raised a fist and knocked on the double wooden doors.

"Come in," came a smooth voice.

Pushing the double doors in, Jayun entered with his head held high. Everything inside matched the outside—yellow wood. From the floors to the walls to the ceiling—everything. It reminded me of Lutum's homes in the sense that everything was constructed using natural resources, but this building was far more polished than anything you'd find in Lutum. The wood was sanded, stained, and covered in something shiny. From the ceiling hung a wooden chandelier with flames dancing from side to side.

The space was smaller than I had anticipated before coming in. But I imagined more rooms sat in the back, where I couldn't see.

"Jayun," came that same voice again.

A man with medium-length brown hair, a short scruff, and a decent build, rounded a wooden corner and approached us at the entrance. His soft brown eyes rolled my way and he smiled—a smile that made me want to trust him.

A few lines spread out on his temples, but they weren't pronounced. The man didn't look old—maybe late thirties or early forties. I wasn't sure. Little orange freckles ran across his cheeks and the bridge of his nose, but they weren't noticeable unless you were looking for them. If anything, it made him look tan.

I wanted to smile back, but instead, I frowned.

I didn't know this man, and I certainly didn't trust him, even if he seemed like a good guy. The last man in authority I'd met had claimed to be my father, and still, he had betrayed me. If a father could betray his own daughter, how could I trust a stranger?

"You must be Silver," the man said.

He ran a hand through his long, clean-looking locks and stared at me, waiting for me to say something."

But I remained tight-lipped.

"I'm Finnigan Wren, but everyone around here calls me Finn." He pressed a calloused hand over his chest and bowed politely.

I wanted to say something along the lines of, "Pleasure to meet you, or thank you for saving me," but instead, I blurted, "What is this place? Why am I here?"

He smiled again, revealing white polished teeth that made me want to close my mouth. He then gave Jayun a look. It was something that translated to, *She isn't the most civilized.*

Maybe I was making things up in my head. Maybe the look had meant something else.

The lines on his face vanished, as did his smile, when Jayun cleared his throat and said, "Sir, we have a problem."

"What is it?" Finn asked.

"The Eye, sir. Penelope spotted it over Death Valley."

Finn's eyes widened slightly, but he immediately composed himself. He cleared his throat and said, "Thank you, Jayun. Let us convene this evening and discuss a course of action."

Closing his eyes, Jayun bowed his head gracefully. "I will be outside."

He turned around and exited through the wooden doors. The moment Jayun left me alone, I swallowed hard, expecting Finn's demeanor to change. Would he now turn into a monster? Scowl at me and tell me to keep my mouth shut?

"May I show you something, Silver?" he asked sweetly.

I nodded.

He moved to the eastern side of the building and rounded a corner, then made his way up an L-shaped staircase. I followed him, admiring the countless paintings on the walls. Many of them were framed in hand-carved wood and showed images of what I assumed was the village in its earlier days, before all the houses were built. The colors were bright— greens, blues, and yellows—and showed people laughing and smiling. The artwork was fascinating, and it made me wish I'd been allowed to learn the arts.

One painting even showed the construction of the strange building I was currently standing in, with only half of the poles in place, barely supporting the home. How had this artwork come about? Had someone stood in the distance, painting what they saw as the construction project took place? I stared at the wall and the countless images, feeling like I was learning the history of the village.

"Do you like it?" Finn asked, spinning his upper body to look at me.

I must have slowed down.

"Um, yes, sorry," I said.

"Don't be," he said and walked toward me, retracing his steps down the staircase.

"This is my favorite." He pointed at the last painting on the wall.

I took a few steps up to see what he was pointing at. Near his finger was a painting of countless men, women, and children, standing in the village and smiling upward as if smiling at the sky.

The details were fascinating, right down to the folds in people's clothing and the sun's rays lightening hair colors in certain spots.

"When was this painted?" I asked.

"Not long ago," he said then laughed as if remembering a funny joke. "It took us about a week to have this created. Lorenzo, our most brilliant painter, assigned everyone positions using nothing but ink and a map, and every day, we stood for hours."

He gazed at the painting as if reliving that week.

"We skipped one day, when it was pouring out, and were cursed with three more days of cloudiness. We stood for hours at a time, and the children became cranky. Despite this, Lorenzo made us look like we were having the best day of our lives." He pointed at the young boy no older than six and let out a soft laugh. "This is Peter. He was the fussiest of the bunch and cried most of the duration."

"He doesn't look sad," I pointed out.

I stared at the toddler who grinned from ear to ear, his bright eyes staring upward as if beaming at a shooting star.

"No," Finn said, his eyes glazing over. "He doesn't."

"Are you in here?" I asked, searching the painting.

"Somewhere," he said, "but I don't recall where." He quickly turned and made his way up the stairs. "Come along."

How would he not remember where he was in the painting? I didn't question him—I got the feeling that he didn't want to talk about it for whatever reason.

I followed him upstairs to the second story, which looked a lot like the first. Everything was yellow and brown, except for a beige fabric sofa that looked so old I wondered if it had come from Grandma's time.

The second I thought of Grandma, I pushed the thought away.

Later, I would cry harder than I'd ever cried before. But right now, I needed to hold myself together. Otherwise, I was afraid I might fall apart and never again be whole.

At the back of the room were windows larger than I'd ever seen. They extended from the floor, all the way to the ceiling, and it was only when Finn reached for the black handle that I realized they were doors.

He smiled back at me and opened the door, allowing a Lilac-scented breeze to sweep through the stuffy space. He stepped out, and I followed him onto the balcony. I wasn't sure where he was taking me, but it seemed like he wanted to show me something.

I craned my neck and stared in awe as I came face-to-face with a mountain's side. Thousands of thick green trees stood tall across its slanted surface. I looked up, but the mountain was so gigantic that I couldn't see its peak from close up.

"Stunning, isn't it?" he asked.

I was too amazed to say anything.

He let out what sounded like a faint laugh and walked around the balcony. "This way."

It led to the side of the building, and beyond it was the field I'd seen earlier—the one in which people had been battling with sticks and wooden weapons. As the late afternoon sun shone down upon them, they fought relentlessly, smacking their weapons together and moving about so fast that I wondered if perhaps they'd been training all their lives.

Some rode on horses, making sharp turns and avoiding obstacles, while others threw weapons, like arrows and spears, at wooden targets.

"They train five times per week," Finn said like a proud father displaying his child's art project.

"Who are they?" I asked.

Finn turned to me and searched my eyes. "Those are our Champions. They're family."

I scrunched my nose. How could anyone

have a family so big?

He must have sensed what I was thinking. He threw his head back and let out a belly laugh. "You still have a lot to learn, Silver. Books can only teach you so much."

I wasn't sure where he was going with this, so I remained silent.

"Family doesn't have to mean blood. Friends can be family."

I'd never read anything about this before, so it was difficult to grasp. In my mind, my mother and grandmother were the only family I had.

His features hardened. "Things aren't the same here as they were in Lutum. No one is a slave here, Silver. You're not a slave anymore. You're free."

The word *slave* penetrated my chest, as did the word *free*.

I'd read one history book that had spoken about slavery, and I remembered thinking to myself that the life I was living felt a lot like slavery. When I brought it up to Grandma, she immediately hushed me and warned me to never speak that word aloud. She said that we should be grateful for the lives we were given and to never question the Elites of Olympus.

But I did question them. All the time.

And now, to find out I was right about them all along made me feel both relieved and saddened.

Finn gently pressed a hand on my shoulder. "You're safe here, Silver."

As I stared into his honey-brown eyes, it was impossible not to believe him. I felt safe—safer than ever before. I turned my head sideways, watching people train down below as they grunted, shouted, and even laughed at times.

I'd heard more laughter since stepping foot inside Ortus than I had in my entire life.

It was difficult to imagine a dangerous place filled with so much happiness.

"You see that?" he asked, pointing at a straight row of young people. They formed a line next to a hay-roofed building and waited patiently. "New recruits."

"Recruits?" I asked. "For what?"

Finn turned to me, a solemn look in his eyes. "For the inevitable, Silver. For war."

I bit my tongue. Hadn't there already been enough bloodshed?

"The Elites will never stop," he said as if reading my mind. "They will continue to rule over Lutum, making people their slaves, and forcing women to produce children like cattle."

I aimed my gaze at the balcony's wooden railing. "I'm not so certain."

Finn leaned against the railing, watching me.

"They threw all of us away," I said. "All of the Breeders."

He stiffened and the balcony creaked. "How—How is that possible?" He turned around and began pacing.

I imagined that if Penelope were here, she'd be better equipped to talk about this. She had, after all, spent many years living as a Breeder.

"I think they've discovered a way to create babies without women," I said.

He rubbed at the brown scruff on his face. "Lab-grown children—"

"I don't know how they do it," I said, but then immediately realized how stupid I must have sounded. Of course, I didn't know—I wasn't a scientist or a doctor.

He stopped pacing and grabbed the railing, his narrowing gaze aimed at the recruits down below. "Then your timing couldn't be better."

What did he mean? And why were there so many recruits if word hadn't yet gotten out about the lab-grown children? Was Finn already planning a war? I didn't understand.

"Is this out of the ordinary?" I asked, pointing at the recruits.

Finn laughed. "Out of the ordinary? We typically receive one recruit every three to four months."

"What changed?" I asked.

Finn smirked, his gaze still fixated on the

lineup of people. "The girl who refused immortality entered our city."

CHAPTER 5

I grew uncomfortable as Finn led me through the village.

Countless heads turned my way, and people stopped talking. Had they been talking about me all along? Why was it such a big deal that I'd refused to become an Elite?

Finn walked with his head held high, his medium-length locks flowing behind him. People bowed with respect as he moved forward, some smiling, others averting their gazes. It was obvious that Finn was a highly respected man in Ortus. I wondered if he was also the founder.

I thought back to the paintings on the wall, and how the first images depicted an empty village with only a few houses. Had he been present when those images were painted? And if so, how long ago was this?

The smell of apples slipped into my nostrils as we walked past the biggest apple tree I'd ever laid eyes on. A young man stood with his young daughter on his shoulders, allowing her to pluck one of the reddest ones hanging low. He grinned so wide with love that his molars made an appearance.

Was this what happiness looked like?

"Over here," Finn said, rounding a small square-shaped house and leading me to another that looked identical.

Strands of hay hung from the rooftop, looking like hair on top of a muffin. The door, also sturdy and likely made of oak, was closed. Finn stepped forward, his boots stomping on the brown cobblestone path, and knocked gently.

At once, a high-pitched voice came soaring out of the open window. "Oh—coming! Coming!"

The front door swung open and out came a woman in a long white and blue dress, her gray hair fastened in a bun at the base of her skull. She was tall—almost as tall as Finn—but very petite looking with tiny wrists and a long neck. Her skin was weathered and almost gray-looking, like she was sick or severely sun-deprived. Her eyes, as gray as her hair, sat above two puffy bags that made me wonder if she'd caught a wink of sleep in the last few days. She squinted at me as if the sight of me hurt her eyes, then took a step back into the safety of her home. Was it me, or was it the sun's reflection? She leaned forward, resting her hands on her dress-covered knees, and said, "You must be Silver."

I tried to smile, but I couldn't. Instead, I nodded and glanced up at Finn. Who was this woman?

"This is Darby," Finn said, smiling sweetly at the older woman.

She beamed at him as if they'd been friends their entire lives. Had they?

"Darby is a dear friend of mine," Finn said, "and I can assure you that you will be safe and comfortable here."

I tried to peer inside the home, but it was too dark. Why were all of her windows closed? It was broad daylight.

She must have sensed what I was thinking. At once, she grinned a set of yellow—almost brown—crooked teeth and said, "Oh, don't mind me. I was only reading. And today is awfully sunny."

Awfully sunny? Since when was the sun such a bad thing?

Finn squeezed my shoulder and I glanced up at him. "Darby suffers from solar urticaria— a rare sun allergy."

I swallowed hard and found myself thinking about all the vampire books I'd read. Every time Darby smiled, I focused on her mouth. Did she have fangs? Was I being ridiculous for even thinking such a thing?

"Thank you, Darby," Finn said. "I know she'll be in good hands." He then turned to me. "I have a meeting to attend now, but I shall see you at supper."

My stomach growled. "Supper?"

"A horn will sound when it's ready," he said. "Supper is always served at the center of the village, next to the statue."

The statue, I remembered.

I hadn't taken much time to look at it, but I recalled seeing a tall stone statue when I first entered Ortus. It had resembled a woman from ancient times—maybe Greek or Roman—wearing a one-shoulder draped dress and carrying a scale. I wasn't sure what it represented, but it must have been significant to be standing in the middle of Ortus.

Finn smiled and turned away before disappearing behind mushroom-shaped houses.

When I looked back at Darby, she beamed as if welcoming a long-lost child.

"Come on in," she said.

I followed her into the darkness of her home, only to be met by three small red wax candles sitting on top of an old kitchen table. Although much smaller than my home in Lutum, which housed five of us, this place was cozy and made me feel safe.

When she caught me staring at the candles, she said, "Three's the maximum amount of candles we're allowed inside."

There were rules here, too, same as in Lutum.

"Supper should be ready in a few hours." She pointed at a small bed with blue cotton sheets that looked brand new. "Why don't you rest your head for a while and I'll wake you when it's time."

I didn't fight her on it. I was beyond exhausted. So I crept into bed, and even though it felt like I had a thousand questions I wanted to ask, I kept my mouth shut and closed my eyes.

At first, it felt like Grandma's touch. It was soft, warm, and loving.

I smiled under my sheets, wondering if maybe Grandma had made something special for breakfast. But the nudging became harder until I snapped my eyes open.

"You sleep like a log," Darby said, her puffy eyes inches away from mine. "Almost thought you wouldn't wake up."

I blinked hard and swallowed, my mouth dry and sticky.

"Here," she said, handing me a glass of water.

I grabbed it, admiring the floral designs carved at the base of the glass.

We didn't have glass in Lutum—only stone dishes and wooden cutlery and utensils.

I chugged it all back and licked my lips. "Thank you."

Darby patted my leg with her veiny hand. "The sun is setting. I'll bring you to the statue."

I followed the old woman as she walked slowly, each step a calculation against the cobblestone path. She clutched onto a straight staff as she moved, her shoulders rounded and her legs wobbly. Poor Darby. I imagined she was in pain, too.

Eyes of all different shapes, sizes, and colors focused on me as I approached the statue. At once, everyone went quiet, almost as if they'd been whispering about me before I showed up. What were they saying? Did they expect me to give some speech? I looked away, feeling out of place.

"Now, now," came Finn's loud voice. He marched through the crowd with arms open wide and his chin up in the air. "Is that any way to welcome our new guest?" He turned to me. "Silver! Come on over. Arahm and his family have made us some food." Finn stepped toward the fire, next to which was a giant cauldron

44

that looked like something out of a fairy tale. Beside the fierce flames were large wooden tables lined up in three rows. Chairs remained tucked underneath the tabletops, waiting for people to sit on them. Finn waved through the air, drawing in the scent of whatever boiled in the cauldron. "Is that your famous pea soup, Arahm?"

Arahm, a middle-aged man with dark features, overly thick brows, dark skin, and a round belly that hung over a rope for a belt, grinned from ear to ear, causing his mustache to widen. It was obvious that he took pride in his food. Around him, five children all about one year apart stood just as proudly, their chins directed at the sky. The youngest of them—a little girl around five years old with big dark eyes—stuck a wooden spoon out at Finn, waiting for him to grab it.

Smirking, Finn jerked his chin sideways at me as if to say, *Come on over*.

With rounded shoulders, I lowered my head, hoping my hair might mask most of my face. I was beyond embarrassed and uncomfortable with the entire village watching my every move. Finn grabbed the little girl's spoon, then reached for a bowl off the table—a white ceramic dish—and handed it over to Arahm. The chef reached into his cauldron with a ladle and scooped out a spoonful of delicious-looking yellow mush. Speckles of black pepper sat on top of the steaming soup and my mouth watered.

"This is your dish now," Finn said, handing me the bowl. He offered me the wooden spoon along with it and the little girl clapped. "You're responsible for keeping it clean. There's a station right over there." He pointed at a stone platform where metal pipes came out of the ground, and a puddle sat at its base.

As I reached for the bowl, a loud, pained cry echoed in the distance.

Everyone's eyes bulged and Finn's head snapped sideways, his intense gaze directed at the village's entrance. He quickly handed me the bowl and I almost spilled it.

"Wait here," he said.

As he ran toward the exit, figures came rushing out of it.

I couldn't see who it was at first. I took a few steps forward and squinted, wanting to move closer.

"Penelope!" Finn shouted. "Medics!"

At once, two men and three women ran from out of the crowd and hurried toward the scene. The first person I recognized was Jayun—he towered over everyone, and in his arms was a limp body.

Penelope?

My friends.

Disobeying Finn's order not to move, I placed my bowl on one of the tables and ran toward them. I needed to know. Had my friends been saved? Had they been harmed?

When Finn stepped aside for the doctors to do their work, I saw her. Penelope lay still with her eyes closed and deep gashes all over her body. Her clothes were torn and stained with dark red blood, as was Jayun's chest and arms.

Jayun's breath was shallow and rapid as he ran a hand first through his beard, then his short curly hair. He looked beyond devastated at the sight of Penelope. "She... she was like this at the door, Finn. I don't even know how she made it back."

Finn clenched his jaw but didn't say a word.

Then, out of the darkness came two familiar faces—Dax and Danika.

"Danika!" I shouted. "Dax!" I ran toward them, but Jayun's big hand got in my way.

"No," he said. "They're in shock. They need time."

"Shock?" I said. "What happened? What's going on?"

I watched in horror as the medics tore layers upon layers of clothing off Penelope, revealing the extent of her injuries. Flesh hung loosely from her body, and on her shoulder was a gash so deep that it revealed some of her muscle.

My stomach sank and I looked away, afraid I might vomit.

"What happened?" I repeated, my voice heightening in pitch.

Jayun's gaze slowly met Finn's, who knelt next to Penelope, holding her hand.

"One alone couldn't have done this," Finn said.

Jayun shook his head. "I agree. But I didn't think they were capable of living in packs."

"Me neither," Finn said.

My eyes darted from side to side as the two men spoke. What were they talking about? Wolves? They couldn't be. Wolves always hunted in packs.

"What can I do?" came an authoritative voice.

I turned around to find an Asian woman with glossy black hair tied into a bun at the back of her head. Her skin was smooth and tanned and her eyes as dark as her hair. She held her pink lips in a flat line as if she held on to no emotion whatsoever. She elevated her chin, revealing a large brown birthmark along the right side of her square jawline. Behind her were dozens of young adults dressed in a similar fashion—dark green clothes with shoulder pads, weapons belts, and leather boots.

"General Reina," Finn said.

He stood up as the medics placed Penelope on some sort of gurney. They raised her into the air and descended toward the cobblestone path before disappearing into the village. Where were they taking her? Was there a medical facility in the village?

Finn moved toward the woman dressed in military attire and placed a hand on her shoulder. "Gather the others, Reina. We have a lot to discuss."

The general nodded, stomped her foot, and shouted, "Retreat!"

The people behind her jogged back toward the fighting grounds I'd seen earlier. When her eyes met Finn's, I knew something was wrong.

"I've never seen anything this bad," Reina said. "How many do you think there were?"

Finn scratched at the light brown scruff on his face. "Those wounds were severe. I'd guess anywhere between three or four, but I can't say for sure." He then turned his attention to Dax and Danika. "We can ask them soon. Right now, let's focus on getting them somewhere safe so we can assess their injuries."

"Injuries?" I tried to get to my friends again, but Jayun kept his hand up.

"Your friends will be fine," he said. "Please, go back to the village."

"I want to know that they're okay!" I shouted.

Finn's eyes rolled toward me. "Silver, please. I know you're concerned, but I promise you that we're doing everything in our power to control the situation."

"Who did this?" I shouted.

I was scared. Terrified, even. I blinked, seeing Penelope's torn body in my mind. What kind of monster could do something like that? Worse—they were speaking as if there were several of them.

Everyone brushed past me as Finn led the group around the outskirts of the village. I couldn't tell if they were going to the fighting grounds or his home.

"Danika!" I called, but she didn't look back.

Instead, Jayun led her forward with a hand on her back, and Dax followed along.

"Please!" I tried, running after them.

Jayun turned around so fast that I stopped in my tracks. He stared me cold in the face, veins bulging from his thick neck. "Listen, child. The less you know about the Daemons, the better. Now go."

Daemons?

He turned back around as I stood silently, feeling like I'd swallowed a bag of rocks.

CHAPTER 6

"Hi, I'm Lyla," came a sweet, feminine voice.

I glanced up from my bowed stance to spot a girl about my age. She stood next to a boy who looked identical to her. Were they related? She beamed, revealing pearly white teeth and dimples in her cheeks. Her hair, a light blond, looked orange as the sun was setting.

"Are you all right?" she asked.

I blinked hard to fight away the daze. What was this? Shock? I didn't know how to feel after what had happened. There had been so much blood. So many wounds.

"Clearly, she isn't," the boy said. "I mean look at her. We should leave her alone."

I stared at the two of them and their light features, feeling like I was seeing fairy tale characters come to life—Hansel and Gretel.

"I think the last thing she needs is to be

51

alone, Lyson. Are *you* looking at her?"

"I *am* looking at her. Don't you have eyes?" Lyson said.

"Are you a twit?" Lyla's brows drew close together. "I'm looking right at you. Of course, I have eyes."

Lyson shook his head and sighed. "Do you want to be alone, or not?" he asked me.

I cleared my throat. "What are *Daemons*?"

Lyson grinned from ear to ear. "She doesn't do small talk. I like her."

Lyla nudged him in the ribs and gave me a worrisome look. "You can't talk about that around here. You'll scare the children."

"But what are they?" I asked.

Lyla's brows furrowed even more dramatically and she grabbed my wrist. "Come on."

They led me behind a house where bumblebees buzzed around tulips.

"How do you even know that word?" she asked. "Most people around here know nothing about that."

"Um, Jayun said it," I said.

She slapped her forehead and rolled her eyes. "That man doesn't know when to stop talking."

I couldn't tell if she was joking or not. Jayun didn't seem like the kind of man who babbled about anything unimportant. If anything, he seemed quiet and reserved.

"They're monsters," Lyla said.

I smirked, imagining one-eyed creatures I'd seen in picture books, but when neither Lyla nor her brother smiled, I realized they weren't trying to be funny.

"What do you mean, *monsters*?" I asked.

Lyla's sky blue eyes doubled in size. "You know... grrr..." She formed claws with her fingers. "Monsters. Kill. Evil." She chewed at the air.

I crinkled my nose and stared at her brother.

"We don't know for sure what they look like," he said, "but I've always heard that they're hairy beasts with teeth longer than a lion's."

"And fangs as sharp as shark teeth," Lyla added.

"Yeah, and they're as big as sharks, too!" Lyson said.

Lyla nudged her brother. "Don't exaggerate. Maybe as big as a lion."

My stomach sank. What the hell were they going on about? It sounded like they were describing mythical creatures that couldn't possibly exist.

"How do you know all of this if no one talks about it?" I asked.

Lyson and his sister exchanged a look—one that told me they weren't even sure where they'd gotten this information.

"Everyone *knows*," Lyson said. "But no one talks about it."

My heart raced. I didn't know what to think. How could such horrid monsters exist? I thought of Penelope and what she must have felt during the attack. She must have been beyond terrified and in so much pain.

My friends, I remembered. Dax, and Danika. And what about the others? Were they still alive? Were they out there with these monsters? I spun around, but Lyla's hand caught my wrist.

"Hey, where are you going?" she asked.

I pulled away. "To get my friends back."

As I rounded one of the houses, I nearly bumped faces with General Reina. Her features barely changed—a bored looked—almost as if she'd been standing there the whole time.

"Going somewhere?" she asked, her eyelids flat.

She stood calmly, waiting for my reaction. Was this a test? Had she been listening to us?

"Actually, yeah," I said. "I need to see Finn."

She clasped her hands together in front of her flat belly and raised her chin. "What for?"

"Only two of my friends came back," I said. "I need to know what happened to the others."

"Great," she said. "Follow me."

She spun around and moved toward the

fighting grounds. I hurried behind her, jogging to keep up. She moved with stiff shoulders as if she were a robot in need of lubrication. We approached a stable with logs fastened together by rope, and the smell of manure filled my nostrils. It reminded me a bit of Lutum—sometimes, the smell of cattle and manure would slip over the wall. We also received shipments of manure for garden fertilizer, and I'd come to love the smell.

Next to the stable stood several horses, most of them brown and white. A few more were inside. In the distance, people rode on other horses, trotting through the field around barrels and jumping over fences.

"Maz," Reina said, approaching a woman with short blond hair, overly tanned skin, and a short, stalky frame.

Maz walked toward us and rolled up her sleeves, revealing white and pink scars up her arms. She didn't seem ashamed of them—if anything, she looked proud, as if these were battle scars. Were they?

She smiled at me when she caught me staring at her arms. "Dogs," she said.

My eyes bulged. She'd been attacked by dogs?

She stuck two fingers inside her mouth and released a high-pitched whistle. At once, three big-headed dogs came running toward her, seemingly from out of nowhere. Two of them were beige with white bellies and short snouts. The other was tall and long-nosed, its coat a blend of black, brown, and white.

The last one, I knew, was a German shepherd. I'd never seen one in real life, but I knew what they looked like. It was frightening to see how large they were—I never imagined dogs to be this big.

Without even being asked, all three of them sat quickly next to Maz and stared up at her as if she held the answers to everything.

"Maz is our K-9 unit trainer," Reina said.

"What are those?" I asked, pointing at the two beige dogs.

"Pit bulls," Maz responded proudly. "Extremely loyal beasts."

The beige dog in the middle looked up at her and its face split into what looked like a huge smile. Although smaller than the German shepherd, they looked incredibly muscular and bulky.

"You can pet them," Maz said.

I hesitated, then decided against it. They had too many sharp teeth for my liking.

Reina leaned into Maz and whispered something, and Maz nodded slowly. Turning around, she whistled again, this time, twice in a row. From behind the stables—where I could only assume was another shelter for dogs—

came two brown creatures with wrinkly skin and huge ears that hung as low as the loose skin from their big snouts.

Bloodhounds, I knew.

They did the same as the other dogs and sat next to Maz.

"Silver, I need to ask for your help," Reina said.

I stared at her.

"Penelope volunteered to be a Searcher when she first came to Ortus several months ago. She hoped to one day be reunited with her friends from Olympus. But she's in critical condition right now, and we have no one else who knows what your friends look like. Would you help with the search?"

I hesitated, wondering how she could ask me to go out there after what had happened to Penelope.

"You wouldn't be going alone," she added. She waved a hand, and four armed fighters—or Champions, as Finn had referred to them—came jogging toward us. Like Penelope, they wore several layers of green and brown clothing that looked unwashed, and on their shoulders were black pads that gave them all the appearance of being bigger than they were. Like the dogs had done, they stopped in front of their leader and watched her silently, never breaking eye contact.

"At ease," Reina said, and they relaxed. "Silver, these are my top four Champions. I can assure you that you'll be safe with them out there."

I made eye contact with the one closest to me—a girl a bit older than me with a face so beautiful I found it hard to look away. She didn't smile and instead eyed me from head to toe with shimmering dark blue eyes. Her cheekbones, high and defined, made her eyes pop even more. She held her head back, allowing her long brown hair to land behind her back, and stared at me like she wanted to punch me in the face. Had I done something to upset her? She was tall—quite a bit taller than me and as tall as the young men beside her—and had an athletic build.

"You can ride with Sadie," Reina said. "She's a great rider and she'll keep you safe."

Sadie broke eye contact with me, her eyes flickering toward Reina. It was like she wanted to protest, to demand that she get to ride alone, but she kept her mouth shut. Instead, she shot me another dirty look that made me feel unworthy.

"I ride fast," she said, matter-of-factly. "I expect you'll hold on."

I didn't respond, and instead looked away.

"Tray, mind the dogs," Maz said.

A young man next to Sadie nodded, his

hands clasped together in front of his belly.

I flinched when Reina grabbed my shoulder. "You've got this," she said. "Nothing will happen to you and you'll be back home in no time."

Home, I thought, my throat swelling.

She must have realized the damage her words had caused. Giving my shoulder a tight squeeze, she forced a smile. "We'll take care of you here, Silver."

I nodded, fighting back tears.

"Come on," came Sadie's cold voice.

Without looking at me, she led me to a brown-and-white horse that looked like the others, only this one had a white diamond between its eyes. She didn't pet the animal or greet it. Instead, she went into the stable and came back out with a saddle. She threw it on the horse's back, tied it up, and climbed on.

I stood awkwardly, not knowing what to do.

She raised her chin. "Are you climbing up, or what?"

I glanced back at Reina.

"Come," Reina said. "Hold here, place your foot there." She pointed, guiding me through the steps. "One, two, three—"

I yanked myself up, clenching my teeth as a throbbing pain shot into my chest. I did my best not to show it. If they knew about my injured ribs, they might not let me go out there looking for my friends. I landed in a small brown leather seat behind Sadie and smiled to myself, proud of my accomplishment. No one else said a word about it. I supposed getting on a horse wasn't a big deal around here.

Reina returned to Maz.

Without warning, Sadie kicked the sides of the horse and it took off, causing me to nearly fall off its rear end.

"I warned you I ride fast," Sadie said. She reached behind her back, grabbed my hand, and placed it on her small waist. "Hold on if you don't want to fall off."

Awkwardly, I placed my other hand on her waist and held on. It gave me butterflies, but I couldn't understand why I felt so nervous. Maybe this rescue mission was more than I could handle. Or, maybe it was Sadie. I couldn't quite put my finger on it, but something about her intimidated me and I wasn't easily intimidated.

I turned my head sideways to spot the entire village looking at us as we moved toward the cavern. People watched us with their spoons in midair, pea soup falling back into their bowls. With her back stiff, Sadie headed forward, leading her horse into the darkness of the cavern.

CHAPTER 7

The horse's hooves kicked rocks in every direction as we strode through Death Valley.

Behind us, the three young men conversed, laughing occasionally. They were too far back for me to hear what they were talking about, but I wondered why Sadie kept such a distance. Why didn't she take part in the conversation? They seemed to be enjoying themselves.

I glanced back to spot the two bloodhounds jogging next to the horses. Despite their droopy, sad-looking faces, they seemed excited to be venturing outside of Ortus. I imagined they didn't get out very much.

"Why are the dogs behind us?" I asked. "I thought bloodhounds had amazing noses."

Sadie ignored me, and I wasn't sure whether to feel stupid or angry. So I bit my tongue as we left Death Valley and entered the lush green field. Every few seconds, Sadie's eyes shot up at the overcast sky. I knew what she was looking for—the Eye, whatever that was. I wanted to question her on it, but I got the feeling she'd ignore me about that, too.

Sadie seemed like the kind of girl who did what she was told and didn't like getting into details. Reina had put her in charge of this mission for a reason, and I wasn't about to question that.

I held on tight to her as the horse gaited toward the forest—the same one in which I'd almost been eaten by wolves. Behind us, the men stopped talking. I imagined they were afraid of the Eye, just as Sadie was.

My eyes shot in every direction as we moved. As much as the Eye freaked me out, I was way more afraid of these Daemon creatures Lyla and her brother had told me about. They'd made them sound like hideous monsters. Were they? Were there other creatures out there I knew nothing about? The only knowledge I had of the real world was what I'd read about in books. What if certain things were too awful to put in books?

I swallowed hard at the thought of a world entirely unknown to me.

This whole time, I'd felt as though all of my reading had given me a road map of the world, or at least a general conception of it. There was so much I knew nothing about, and it terrified me.

My stomach formed knots as I bounced up and down in my saddle, envisioning a gruesome attack.

You'll be safe. I remembered Reina's words. She must have been certain of this to speak it aloud. Finn had welcomed me into Ortus as if my very existence was going to change everyone's lives. No way would they risk losing me at this point. Right?

We slowed as we entered the forest, Sadie bending her upper body every few minutes to avoid hitting a large branch. She didn't warn me, either, and at one point, a sharp branch scratched my cheek, splitting it open.

"You could have warned me," I grumbled, unable to keep my mouth shut.

She didn't answer, and I could have sworn I heard her chuckle at the front.

I wasn't sure how I felt about this girl, or if I'd ever grow to like her. I thought back to Star and how off-putting she'd seemed when I first met her, but I'd quickly grown to like her. Sadie seemed like the type of person who held on to a lot of anger for whatever reason and felt pleasure when others suffered.

A real psychopath.

You know nothing about her, I reminded myself.

If Grandma were here, she'd tell me not to

be so quick to judge. Often, she'd even defend Mother for acting like a real monster. Why? She said Mother had been through a lot, and although her behavior was at times unacceptable, she was human and she was damaged. I missed Grandma more than anything.

"What the hell are you doing?" Sadie asked.

What *was* I doing? I'd been so lost in thought over Grandma that I'd tightened my grip around Sadie's waist, hugging her. Embarrassed, I immediately pulled away.

"Sorry," I blurted. "I thought I saw something and got scared."

The reason I gave her made me feel even smaller. *Scared?* I was supposed to be a beacon of hope for the people of Ortus. It was stupid of me to express fear.

"Well, stop it," she said. "I'm not here to comfort you."

I cleared my throat, feeling my cheeks warm to an unpleasant shade of red. A gust of wind swept through the forest, sending a flowery scent up my nostrils. It calmed me instantly, and I inhaled deeper, taking it all in. I wasn't sure if it had come from flowers, or Sadie's long hair in the wind, but it smelled nice.

"I need you to keep your mouth shut over here," she said.

64

I parted my lips, prepared to argue that I wasn't even talking, when she kicked the sides of her horse and we exited the forest. To my left was the giant cliff I'd tumbled down. At the top of it were the train tracks, though I couldn't see them from here. My ribs throbbed painfully at the sight of the steep drop. Eventually, I'd have to get them looked at. How bad was the damage? Had I cracked them? Broken them? Or were they simply bruised? Every breath hurt, and even the horse ride, made me gnash my teeth together.

Sadie slowed down, shaking me from my thoughts. Up ahead, at the base of the cliff, were jagged rocks and massive boulders that looked like the kind of spot the Elites would aim for. To my surprise, there was no blood or any evidence of injury. I swallowed hard, realizing that if they'd waited a few more seconds to throw me out of the train, my brains might have splattered all over those rocks.

Sadie pointed at the ground, and I followed her finger. In the tall grass were prints—not obvious prints in the mud, but flattened grass that told me someone had walked here.

"See that?" She pointed again, this time at speckles of blood. "Likely Penelope's, which means she found your friends not far from here."

Although I assumed Dax and Danika had

been tossed out before Echo, Rose, and Asako, I couldn't be sure. Maybe the others had taken off or landed somewhere hidden, making it impossible to find them.

Either that, or they'd been killed, and their bodies dragged away.

I cringed at the thought and willed it away.

We continued several miles along the base of the cliff as chills ran up my spine. Every few feet, blood sat at the tips of the grass blades. How far had Penelope traveled with her injuries? Had she remained on her horse, or had she fallen off?

My gaze shifted toward the darkening clouds.

The Eye—or whatever it was Greer had spoken of—what was it? And were we in danger?

Sadie snapped her fingers, and behind us, Tray hissed, "Search."

At once, the two bloodhounds charged straight ahead, their floppy ears nearly touching the ground as they swayed in every direction, following a scent.

They led us around the cliff's bend, near another forest made up mostly of pine trees and dirt. But they didn't go inside the forest— they continued sniffing alongside the cliff, around boulders and bushes.

One of them barked, and the other did the

same. It was a deep, consistent bellow—almost a howl. Sadie kicked her horse, propelling us forward, and approached the two howling creatures.

A faint whimper slipped out from between two bushes and a pair of white sneakers attached to two dark legs kicked at the dogs' snouts. They didn't growl or bare their teeth. Instead, they backed away and waited for us to approach.

"Heel," said Tray, coming up beside us.

The dogs backed away even further as Sadie moved in. As we got closer, the little legs disappeared into the bushes.

"It's okay," Sadie said. "We're here to help."

No response.

I squinted at the bushes, hoping to catch a glimpse of a familiar face.

"Hello?" I said.

Sadie gave me a nasty look—one that told me to keep my mouth shut unless otherwise instructed.

"Come out," Sadie ordered, her tone cold.

Another faint, high-pitched whimper.

Then, I caught a glimpse of dark, frizzy hair and brown skin. The bushes rustled as the person tried to hide deeper inside.

Sadie clicked her fingers again and two of the Champions behind us—one blond boy with alabaster white skin and another with dark features—climbed off their horses and moved toward the hideout.

Sadie jerked her chin, and although she didn't say anything, I knew exactly what she'd ordered: get that person out of there.

The two boys reached inside and the whimpering amounted to a faint cry. It was a pleading sound that begged them to let her go. The second they managed to pull her out, I saw her face and my heart skipped a beat.

"Rose!"

I was about to swing my leg behind me and jump off the horse when Sadie's hand smacked my shoulder. She turned, the equipment around her waist making a squeaking sound against the saddle. "No, you stay."

"But I know her," I said. "I can help."

Rose stared up at me, looking petrified. Her huge brown eyes shot between me and Sadie as if she were trying to figure out whether or not any of this was even real. Her right cheek looked severely bruised, and part of her shirt was torn near her abdomen. It was obvious she'd caught a few nasty rocks on the way down. As I stared at her small, pointed features, I couldn't help but feel devasted for her. Ever since I'd met Rose, she hadn't uttered a word. I imagined she had a thousand questions for us, but she would never voice them aloud.

"It's okay," I said. "They're here to help us."

This seemed to calm her. She stopped struggling and stood still, her tiny sticks for arms held firmly by the Champions.

"Dax and Danika are safe, too," I added.

Her lips parted, but nothing came out. She swallowed hard, nodded, and bit her bottom lip.

"Adam, take her back," Sadie ordered.

The dark-featured boy nodded and led Rose to his horse.

"The rest of us will keep searching," Sadie said.

I felt awful watching Rose get placed on the horse. She looked beyond mortified, and why wouldn't she be? Aside from me, everyone here was a stranger to her, and now, she was being taken to some unknown village with some guy she knew nothing about. Adam kicked his ankles into his horse's sides and they took off.

Rose twisted her neck to keep looking at me, her pleading eyes begging me not to take too long.

"I'll see you soon!" I said as they strode off into the open field.

CHAPTER 8

We continued our journey several more miles around the cliff. Eventually, the tracks overhead disappeared over a long bridge across a river. As I stared at the distant water, I wondered if maybe the Elites had been cruel enough to throw someone into the water.

Then again, maybe this would have been better than throwing someone onto jagged rocks.

We hadn't found anyone else yet, and I was beginning to wonder if maybe we were too late. What if the Daemons had gotten to Echo? To Asako? What if they'd torn them apart as they'd tried to do to Penelope?

Sadie pulled on the reins of her horse and led us toward the ominous forest. It was vast and appeared to be never-ending.

"You can't go in there," Tray said behind us.

Sadie shot him a death glare.

"I'm not an idiot, Tray," she said. "I know the rules."

"Rules?" I said.

Sadie yanked sideways on her reins and trotted along the forest's perimeter.

"Why can't we go in?" I asked.

"Daemon territory," she said.

"You think Penelope went inside? Is that why she got attacked?" I asked.

Sadie sighed like I was nothing more than an annoying toddler asking for playtime.

"Penelope didn't go inside," she said. "She knows the rules like everyone else."

"Then why are we riding so close to the forest? What if the Daemons come after—"

"Let them try," she growled. "We'll be the last thing they ever lay eyes on."

She gripped a spear that stood pointed up against her saddle. It looked to be made of finely carved wood and bone, with rope holding everything together. Sadie wasn't afraid of a fight. I wasn't sure whether she was brave or delusional.

I thought back to Penelope and how torn up she'd been. Whatever she'd gone up against was dangerous. I, for one, didn't want to taunt these monsters.

"Penelope isn't a fighter," Sadie said. "Whatever happened today was a freak accident. I promise, you're safe with me."

I felt somewhat relieved but didn't say anything. It was the nicest thing she'd said to me since I'd met her, and I didn't want to push my luck.

We galloped a bit farther, riding through the tall trees' shadows, when Sadie said, "I hate to break it to you, but if your other friends aren't out here, they're as good as dead."

Why was she telling me this? I parted my lips to question her, when she added, "Anyone who's ever gone into that forest has never been seen again. And we've searched the area. They must have gone into the forest."

I swallowed hard and began searching the open space around me. I searched for skin, clothing, anything. Maybe we just hadn't seen them. I hoped that neither Echo nor Asako had stepped foot inside that forest. I didn't want to imagine what might have happened to them if they did.

The farther we rode, the more hopeless I felt. The forest's perimeter ran long—countless miles—before curving and redirecting us toward Death Valley again. The dogs ran around, sniffing the air and ground and running in zigzags. It was obvious they didn't smell anything.

"Sorry," Sadie said. "They aren't out here."

"Can we look one more time?" I asked.

My grip involuntarily tightened around her

waist as I waited for her answer.

She remained stiff and silent, until finally, she said, "We can do one last sweep."

I wanted to thank her, but I was afraid if I showed any sort of kindness, she'd scoff at me or tell me to shut up. So I held on to her as we cut through the open field and raced back toward the cliff. Overhead, thunder cracked, and I flinched.

"Let's do this quickly," Sadie shouted.

The bloodhounds went at it again, sniffing wildly as rain sprinkled from above. Would the weather interfere with the dogs' ability to smell or enhance it? They didn't seem bothered by the rain. It was light and warm and tickled the back of my neck.

I searched the tall grass, hoping to spot something no one else had seen.

But as the dogs zigzagged, searching for something that wasn't there, my heart sank. What had happened to Echo? To Asako? Had they been slaughtered? Had their bodies been taken away by wolves? My throat swelled at the thought. Although I didn't know them well, these women were the closest things to friends I'd ever known.

We sped near the cliff again, this time at a greater distance to cover more ground. Sadie was about to change direction again when Tray whistled, pulling my attention toward him and the dogs. They ran toward something, flattening the tall grass as they hunted.

"They found something," Sadie said. She sped up, joining Tray and the dogs about half a mile away from the forest's perimeter.

It wasn't until we drew in nearer that I spotted a small pond surrounded by an abundance of cattails. The ground surrounding the water was damp and cold-looking. The horses didn't seem to appreciate the squishy texture. Sadie's stepped back when our horse's hooves sank into the muddy area.

"Wait here," she said.

She hopped off and landed hard, mud splattering into the air.

Tray ordered the dogs to back away and Sadie moved cautiously, her hand hovering over what appeared to be a bone knife on her belt. She pushed aside several cattails and bent down, disappearing almost entirely.

When she stood back up, she looked at me and shook her head. "She's gone."

Using the saddle's footrests, I pushed my body up, hoping to catch a glimpse. Who was it? Who was gone? I couldn't see anything.

"Tall, brunette," she said.

Echo.

Slowly, I sat back in the saddle, feeling defeated.

I wanted to ask if she was injured, but I'd

seen enough for one day. My mind was already clouded with so many awful thoughts that I feared no more could fit. I shook my head as a way of saying, *Okay, let's keep moving*, when something hot flew by my face and a loud swooshing sound deafened my right ear.

It had happened so fast that at first, I didn't feel the pain.

It took a split second for my cheek to begin throbbing, but I didn't have time to reach for it. Without warning, my horse shot upright, neighing wildly and kicking its front legs in the air. Unlike last time, I didn't allow myself to fall off. I held on, hugging the saddle's front seat as tight as I could.

"Silver!" Sadie shouted.

The horse came back down with a thump, causing my face to smash into its back.

But I held on.

Another swoosh sound filled the sky, and I snapped my head sideways to spot a fire arrow smothered in the grass. The flames went out almost immediately, but the sight of it formed knots in my stomach.

The dogs barked and howled as the other two horses stood on their hind legs. Shouting erupted behind me, while Tray and the other two young men tried to get a grip of their horses.

Sadie reached for her horse's reins, fighting

with its massive swaying head.

"Hold still!" she shouted.

Without warning, several more arrows came pouring from the sky, zipping through the rain and landing hard around us.

Tray let out a cry, his mouth a gaping hole. From his stomach protruded an arrow, its feathered end bright and colorful. Around its sharp point, however, was dark blood soaking through Tray's clothing.

"Tray!" the other young man shouted.

"Retreat!" Sadie shouted.

She managed to climb back on and kick the horse's side just as another dozen arrows came raining from the clouds. They landed right where I'd been only seconds ago, and my heart skipped a beat.

"Hiya!" Sadie shouted, kicking hard again.

We galloped so fast that my hair flew behind me and I squinted to prevent rain from hurting my eyes. Behind us, Tray followed us awkwardly, his body slanted sideways as he held on to the arrow in his belly.

His skin, pale and gray, made him look like he was about to die any second.

His friend tried to guide him, shouting through the rain every few seconds and pointing straight ahead, no doubt telling him to follow Sadie.

We swept through the field at lightning

speed as thunder roared from above. I worried that by the time we made it back to Death Valley, Tray would be gone.

Surprisingly, he held on.

When we entered Death Valley, all sound seemed to disappear. The mountains around the valley offered a barrier, calming me instantly.

Were we still under attack? Were we being chased? I glanced behind me every few seconds at the heartbreaking sight of Tray and his dogs. He seemed to slant even more now, his eyelids fluttering and his jaw hanging slack.

Sadie led us right past Ortus's entry point and continued down the valley.

"Where are we going?" I asked.

Finally, she slowed.

"Following protocol," she said.

"Protocol?" I asked.

Out of breath, she said, "We were just attacked, Silver. Do you really think it's smart to lead our enemies straight to our village?"

I didn't respond. I realized how idiotic it would have been to run into the tunnel. If our enemies were close behind, we risked everyone's lives inside of Ortus.

We continued riding between the mountains, mud splashing under us. In the distance came the sound of a waterfall. It was light and pleasant sounding, like water cascading off smooth rocks. We rounded a corner and a damp scent filled my nostrils.

Where were we going?

Sadie turned again, this time, guiding us toward a wall of leaves and vines against a stone wall. It was the strangest thing I'd ever seen.

She whistled once, then twice, and the wall shifted sideways.

Two brown, black-outlined eyes appeared in the crack, widening the moment they landed on Sadie.

"Sadie!"

The wall of leaves shifted sideways, revealing a small-framed man with well-groomed hair and a pretty face. He wore a leather vest with a deep V-cut that descended halfway down his abdomen. The lower half of his body was covered with tight leather pants that accentuated his tiny frame. Around his neck was a necklace formed of colorful beads—something likely crafted and gifted by a child. He stared at us, his eyes darting from side to side as if assessing the threat level.

"Elijah," Sadie said, catching her breath. "I think we outran them."

"What the hell happened?" the man—Elijah—asked.

Despite the scowl on his face, his voice was sweet and his mannerisms feminine.

Sadie must have given him an impatient look. Elijah immediately pushed the barrier even farther to the side and urged us inside. Tray's horse trotted past us and into the secret area as if it knew its master needed immediate attention.

"Arrow to the abdomen," Sadie said. "He needs help. Now."

Elijah nodded and ran backward, shouting at people nearby. He flailed his arms over his head as he gave orders.

As we entered the space, I blinked hard.

It wasn't large—maybe a quarter of the size of my division in Lutum—and felt dark and dreary, with tall mountains forming a barrier around us. Overhead, dark clouds floated, making everything that much darker.

Baskets of fruits and vegetables sat in the center near a smothered fire, shimmering with rainwater.

Two women ran to Tray and helped him off his horse. He stumbled, nearly knocking everyone over, but managed to regain his footing. The women led him inside a shallow cave, or a groove, carved out of the mountain's base. It created an overhead canopy, protecting everything underneath from the rain.

Several beds lay against the back wall, and next to them were lit torches dancing from side to side. The only reason they were still burning was because of the overhead canopies—some naturally carved in stone, others made of thick suede and wooden posts.

They brought Tray to one of the beds as more people approached, prepared to tend to his wounds.

"What happened?" Elijah asked, returning to us.

He planted two bony hands on his waist and glared at Sadie with more attitude than she had given me. I couldn't tell whether these two were enemies or best friends.

"D-d-aemons," I said. "Right?"

Sadie crossed her arms and shook her head. "Those weren't Daemons."

"Clearly," Elijah said, letting his mouth hang open.

What did he mean, *clearly*? How did he know what had attacked us? It wasn't like he had been there.

His dark-outlined eyes turned on me. "Who's this? A new recruit?"

He wasn't nice about it, either. I wondered if he and Sadie were related. Their hair color was almost an exact match.

"This is Silver," Sadie said without looking at me.

"Silver?" Elijah said. "Is that supposed to tell me something? What the hell were you thinking bringing a recruit out in the field?"

Sadie tightened her arms over her chest and breathed out hard through her nostrils. She didn't have to say anything for Elijah to tone the attitude down. His eyes went big, and the two of them exchanged a moment that led me to believe they were communicating telepathically.

"Oh. Oh!" Elijah said. "Silver! As in, *the* Silver?"

Sadie rolled her eyes but flinched when Elijah slapped her shoulder. "That's even worse!" he shouted. "What's wrong with you? Why would you bring the girl out? I mean, Finn's been wanting to meet—"

"It wasn't my idea," Sadie growled. "It was Reina's. We needed her to identify survivors."

He pushed his cheek with his tongue, likely holding back countless words.

"Did you see them?" he asked.

Sadie shook her head.

Them? What was he talking about?

"But the arrow confirms it," she said.

I peered toward Tray as he lay still, surrounded by people trying to remove the arrow from his body.

"Who did that?" I asked. "The Elites?"

Sadie shook her head. "Woodfaces."

I blinked hard. "*Woodfaces?*"

Elijah pinched the bridge of his nose,

breathed out hard, then slapped the air. "This doesn't make any sense. I thought we had a treaty with that tribe."

"We did," Sadie said. "And now we don't."

CHAPTER 9

Sadie and I sat under another canopy-like hole in the mountain, watching flames dance near the tips of our toes.

"You cold?" she asked.

I shrugged. As much as I wanted more heat, I didn't want to come across as demanding. It was apparent that Sadie wasn't the type to comfort anyone. She'd outright told me earlier.

"It's either yes or no," she said bluntly.

"A bit," I admitted.

She removed a fur shawl from around her shoulders and placed it around mine.

"Thanks," I mumbled.

"Don't mention it." She poked a stick into the fire, causing embers to float into the air and toward the starlit sky.

"What are Woodfaces?" I asked.

For a moment, she kept tight-lipped, and I figured she'd ignore me again. I was getting accustomed to her strange and rude demeanor.

"Another tribe," she said, poking the fire again. Her glossy blue eyes looked green behind the fire's orange glow. "Savages, if you ask me."

She seemed bitter—hateful, even.

She prodded again, this time, causing a log to fall into the dirt next to the firepit. "I don't agree with the treaty, but it wasn't mine to make."

"Treaty?" I asked.

Pulling her knees up to her chest, she sighed. "They live on the other side of the river—past the bridge you saw earlier. They used to cross the river for resources, but it often led to fights between our people. Finn finally made a truce with their leader, and they agreed to remain on their side of the river in exchange for metal."

"So why were they out in the field today?"

Sadie shook her head. "I don't know. Finn can deal with it."

"Do you hate them?" I asked.

She turned her head to look at me, and I swallowed hard at the sight of her. Her beige skin, dirty and stained, didn't take away from her beauty. If anything, it made her eyes stand out even more.

She had a long face with striking features, and a small pink scar above her right eyebrow.

Her hair was wet and frizzy from today's rain, looking almost black, but I didn't pay much attention to that. She narrowed her eyes on me as if trying to get a look inside my head, and my stomach sank. I couldn't tell whether her gaze meant she was lost in thought or telling me to back off.

I directed my focus into the fire. "You don't have to talk about it if you don't want to."

"Good," she said, "because those savages aren't worth my breath."

She tossed the stick next to the fire and stood up. "You'd better get some rest. We'll make our way back to the village tomorrow."

She lowered herself onto a small, stained mattress against the mountain's stone wall and turned away from me. Only a few inches thick, it looked even more uncomfortable than the hay I used to sleep on in Lutum. The second mattress was positioned a few feet away from hers, so I lay down and curled up into the fur shawl she'd given me.

I woke to the sound of water pouring gently into a cup.

"Drink up," Sadie said, smashing a stone cup next to my bed.

I blinked hard, my crusted eyes heavy and

dull.

"Rise and shine, sleeping beauties!" Elijah came at us, his hips swaying from side to side. Under the morning light, his eyes looked even more outlined than the night before.

"There's fruit near Polly over there, if you're hungry. Or fish. Not everyone likes fish for breakfast, but"—he extended both arms on either side of him, widening the V-cut on his chest and exposing his tiny nipples—"we've got an unlimited supply, baby."

I caught the scent of fresh water. Although I couldn't see it with the wall closed, I could hear a powerful river nearby.

"Go on," he said, urging us up. "Get up. Eat. And then get the hell out of here."

Sadie rolled her eyes, but a hint of a smile tugged at her lips. It warmed me, making me wish she'd smile more often.

"Elijah, forever the optimist," she said.

"What's there not to celebrate, darling?" He grabbed his hips. "You're all alive, and Tray survived the night."

Sadie shot upright as if she'd forgotten entirely about Tray's injuries. "How is he?"

Elijah's smile vanished. "He's stable for now. We sent him back to Ortus early this morning with the other two. I'm sure they're expecting you soon, too. The boat's ready whenever you are."

"Boat?" I said. "What about the horses?"

Elijah smirked at me. "Have some faith, love. We've been doing this for a while. The horses will be returned in a few days once we're certain Death Valley is clear."

There was a flirtatious way about him, making it difficult not to like him.

Sadie moved toward him, wrapped an arm around his shoulders, and said, "We'll eat in Ortus. Stay safe, Elijah."

She kissed his forehead before moving toward a small opening in the mountain. The hole looked narrow—maybe the size of a doorway—through which light escaped.

"You too, darling," he said. "Oh, and Silver_-"

I turned around, but Sadie kept walking.

"Do make a fuss for me, won't you?" he said. I must have grimaced at him, not knowing what he was talking about. He let out a soft chuckle and twirled a finger in the air. "Stir shit up in Ortus. God knows we need a change around here."

I still wasn't sure what he meant, so I nodded politely and raced toward Sadie. She squeezed through the narrow passageway, leading us onto a small wooden platform next to a dark blue river with a powerful current. The platform swayed as the current swept underneath it, forming bubbles and foam.

"Come on." She hopped onto the platform,

seemingly unbothered by its unsteadiness.

At the other end was a wooden canoe. It was much larger than what I had envisioned a canoe might look like, which comforted me. With one end fastened to the dock, it remained in place, moving only slightly as the water slipped underneath.

Sadie offered me a hand to help me in. Her touch was firm and warm and made me feel secure. I lowered myself into the boat, my stomach queasy. When Sadie stepped inside, I feared the additional weight might cause us to dip underneath the water, but the canoe remained afloat.

"First time?" she asked.

I nodded.

"You get used to it."

She reached toward the dock, unfastened a large rope, and pushed us into the river.

"Watch out." She brushed past me, her soft hair tickling my cheek, and grabbed a large wooden stick from the bottom of the canoe.

"Paddle," she said, showing me the large stick.

She dipped it into the water and pushed, causing us to float away from the shore. I watched in admiration as she steered the boat with the strange-looking paddle.

Slowly, the morning sun slipped between two mountains, warming my face. As we floated quietly, I smiled up at the now-cloudless sky and felt at peace for the first time in as long as I could remember. The water's current propelled us forward, relaxing me, and every few seconds, Sadie used the paddle to correct our course.

Every time she paddled, it created a soft swooshing sound that made me want to close my eyes and fall asleep. So I lay back in the canoe, my head propped up on a piece of wood that ran horizontally across the bottom.

"Just rest, princess. I'll take care of the heavy lifting," Sadie said.

I glanced back at her. Had this been a joke? Why was she calling me *princess*? Her tone made me think she was being sarcastic. "Sorry—did you want me to help?"

"No," she said without looking down at me.

What was up with her? I couldn't tell what she was thinking or what she meant when she said certain things. Granted, I didn't have much experience with social interaction, having grown up in Lutum. But I got the feeling that she was purposely trying to make me feel bad. Either that, or she needed to make it a point that she didn't think I was special the way everyone else thought.

Was it jealousy? Maybe.

I stared at the blue sky as birds of all different wingspans flew above. Some cawed, others sang, and I became entranced by their melodies. In Lutum, hearing birds sing was a rarity. I smiled up at them, forgetting all of my problems.

"What do you have to be so chipper about?" Sadie asked.

Was she watching me? I blinked hard, my cheeks warming uncomfortably.

"Um, just the birds," I said. "They're beautiful."

She scoffed. "They're just birds."

Two small birds with blue feathers swept over our heads, pecking wildly at each other. Neither one chirped out in pain, so I assumed they were playing. It made me smile.

"Maybe to you," I said. "You see birds all the time. But to me, this is special."

She ignored me, which came as no surprise.

As I continued to watch the birds, I remembered the Eye that had flown over Death Valley.

"What's the Eye?" I asked.

She stopped rowing and rested the wet paddle across her lap.

"How do you know about that?" she asked.

I sat upright and was met by her penetrating eyes. "I overhead Penelope," I said. "She was talking to Jayun. And I saw it, too. It flew over Death Valley."

Sadie clenched her jaw and looked away.

Was I upsetting her? Had I said something I shouldn't have?

"What's wrong?" I asked.

"Nothing," she said coldly.

She was lying. In the few hours I'd spent with Sadie, I'd come to learn that she did as she wanted, and no one could tell her otherwise. If she didn't want to talk about it, she wouldn't.

"And we aren't sure what it is," she said.

I wasn't sure what she meant by that.

"The Eye," she clarified. "We don't know what it is. We think it's some sort of monitoring system designed by the Elites. It usually circles the train tracks a day or two after drops are made. It's almost like it flies around to make sure no one survives the fall. Either that, or it's monitoring the Daemons."

"Well, I survived," I said.

"Exactly." She sounded upset by this. "Maybe that's why the Eye is traveling farther than usual. It's probably looking for you."

I swallowed hard. Looking for me? What did it want with me? Could it hurt me? And what did the Daemons have to do with this?

"Are they really monsters?" I asked.

She snorted like I was a complete moron. "Depends on your definition of monsters."

I shrugged. How was I supposed to describe a monster? I'd seen all sorts of depictions on paper, but I'd never seen one in real life.

"Let me guess," she said, "you talked to someone in the village about it."

How did she know? I kept the twins' names—Lyla and Lyson—out of my mouth.

"If you want real information, don't ask the citizens," she said.

She spoke of the citizens as if they were a different people. Were they? To her?

"There's a lot they don't know," she continued. "That also means that you'd better keep your mouth shut about the Eye."

I sensed her glare lingering on me. "You haven't told anyone, have you?" she asked.

I sat upright and twisted my neck to look at her. "About what? The Eye? No."

"Good," she said. "Keep it that way. People don't know about that thing. If they did, it would be chaos. So you'd better keep your trap shut."

"Okay, I get it," I said sharply. I was getting tired of the way she spoke to me. I didn't understand what reason she had to hate me so much, and it was beyond frustrating.

"Good," she said, no doubt wanting to get that last word in.

We sat in silence for a while longer as we rounded a mountain full of trees. In the distance came a crackling sound, and it wasn't until I searched the distant trees that I saw them—four-legged animals hopping around in the mountains. They were white and fluffy-looking, with black horns protruding from the tops of their heads.

It made me smile. Sadie didn't seem to care.

"What are those?" I asked.

She looked at me like I was stupid. "Mountain goats."

It wasn't long before I spotted grass in the distance, and then, hay rooftops.

"Is that Ortus?" I asked, stiffening.

Sadie didn't answer, which I assumed was her way of saying, *Obviously.*

She guided the canoe toward a wooden platform over the water held in place by sturdy posts. She paddled hard to get us out of the current, making it obvious that she'd done this several times over. When the front of our canoe collided gently with the wooden platform, she reached her long arms toward one of the posts and grabbed a rope.

Within minutes, the canoe sat flush against the structure and Sadie urged me to get out.

"This is called a *dock*, by the way," she said.

I grabbed one of the posts for support, but as I climbed out, the tip of my shoe caught the wooden ledge and I fell onto my knees. Instantly, pain shot up into my rib cage and I cried out.

Sadie jumped out like a mother tending to

her injured child and knelt next to me, a hand on my back. "You okay? What's wrong?"

Although I wanted to hide my pain, my hand had a mind of its own and instinctively reached for my abdomen. Without even asking for my permission, Sadie grabbed my arm, raised it high, and lifted my shirt to reveal my ribs.

"You're hurt," she said. "When did this happen?"

"When I got thrown off the train," I said, wincing.

"Lie down," she ordered.

I hesitated, but her big blue eyes warned me that it was in my best interests to listen.

So I rolled over onto my back and lay still, the sun warming my bare stomach. She yanked my shirt up even higher and ran her fingers along my ribs, assessing the damage. Her touch made my entire body tingle. I'd never had physical contact with anyone other than my mom—which was always unpleasant—and the occasional hug or shoulder squeeze from my grandmother.

Her warm touch made me feel weak and hypnotized despite my pain.

"Does this hurt?" She pressed into my ribs and I winced. "How about here? And here?" Her hot breath blew against my belly as she spoke, causing goose bumps to erupt all over my body. For a split second, I froze, unable to respond. She tucked loose hair behind her ear and stared at me. For the first time, she wasn't looking at me like she wanted me dead.

But the moment was brief—she cleared her throat, made her eyes go big, and said, "Well?"

"Um, yeah, it hurts a bit."

She continued poking at me and watching for a reaction until finally, she yanked my shirt back down. "Bruised ribs," she said. "You'll be fine in a few weeks. Get up."

She rose before me and left the dock. I blinked hard a few times, trying to shake the daze I'd fallen into.

When I didn't follow right away, she stopped walking and said, "Are you coming, or what?"

CHAPTER 10

I followed Sadie as she took long strides toward two large wooden gates. On either side of the gates was a tall wooden fence constructed of thick logs. The top end of each log was sharp, like someone had spent days carving it into a fine point. It made me thankful not to be an enemy of Ortus.

The barrier seemed never-ending, following the river's bend until it disappeared.

On either side of these gates were strange-looking buckets that seemed to float in the air behind the fence. I imagined they stood on posts. As we drew in nearer, two heads poked out—one out of each bucket.

The man on the right stood proudly with a helmet over his head, his gaze aimed at Sadie, while the man on the left rubbed his eyes as if he'd been taking a nap in there.

Sadie didn't say anything. Instead, she walked right up to the gates and waited. Both men reached for something around waist height. A knocking sound echoed from behind the gates and they creaked open.

Sadie led me through, but as we entered Ortus, something felt off. When I'd first arrived at the village, the entire place had buzzed with voices and laughter. Now, everything was silent.

"Where is everyone?" I asked.

I jogged to catch up to Sadie who marched past empty garden beds and the school's playground.

"I don't know," she admitted.

She moved even faster, making it nearly impossible for me to keep up with my injured ribs. If I ran too fast, the bounce in my body caused a throbbing pain.

The more we walked, the more it became obvious that the village had become deserted.

Where was everyone? How could so many people disappear so quickly? The day prior, people had been roaming around everywhere—the fighting grounds, the village, and the small courtyard where the Greek statue stood. Where were all the children? I'd seen them playing next to the school, near the apple trees.

I swallowed hard as knots formed in my stomach. Had the Eye made its way over? Had the village been attacked?

"What's going on? Where is everyone?" My voice came out quaky this time.

Sadie stopped walking, grabbed her hips, and sighed. "Likely at the Path of Departure."

"Path of Departure?" I said.

She bowed her head. I was about to ask her what was wrong, when she rounded the garden beds and said, "Follow me."

She led me past the agriculture area, where chickens roamed freely and a dozen cows lay in the field. It filled the air with a farm smell that I loved, and it made me think of Lutum.

Behind the animals was a wooden barn with bales of hay around its weathered exterior. Its massive doors sat open, held firmly in place by bricks in the dirt. From the darkness within came the faint sound of pigs grunting.

The cows raised their large heads as we moved past them, but they didn't seem bothered by our presence. We made our way along the fighting grounds' barrier—which looked a lot like the fence used to separate Ortus from the river—and descended a gentle slope.

About halfway down, I saw them— countless people gathered in a small, open field next to the river. The fence that had kept me out of Ortus reached down here as well, extending to the mountain's side. It seemed to keep everyone safe inside of Ortus. Men, women, and children stood quietly, watching something near the water. On the other side of the gates were a few people walking toward the river carrying a platform of some sort.

"No," Sadie breathed.

Without warning, she ran down the slope on an angle, careful not to tumble down. A few heads turned to her as she breathed loudly, but no one spoke. She ran through the crowd, shoving people aside, and raced through the set of open gates.

Although not quite as fast as her, I managed to keep up and met her on the other side. By the time I got there, she stood at the edge of the river with arms crossed over her belly and a bowed head.

Without a word, the people who had been carrying the platform lowered it into the grass, revealing a still, lifeless body.

But it wasn't just any body.

It was Penelope's.

She lay peacefully, her dull skin having changed to a light shade of gray. In her grasp were poppies—a vibrant red that matched the gashes all over her arms—and covering her was a white cotton sheet. Over her closed eyelids were metallic coins with smooth edges and symbols I couldn't make out.

One of the men turned around—Finn. He gave me a solemn look but didn't say a word.

I watched, my heart throbbing, as Finn and three other men reached for the platform again and lowered it into the water. Finn rolled up his pant legs and stepped into the river, finding his footing against river stones. Dark water licked his bare ankles as he moved in deeper, pushing Penelope's wooden bed into the water. A gentle breeze swept across the river, causing a few strands of Penelope's hair to get stuck on her lips.

Not that it mattered. She couldn't feel it. She was dead. Gone. Forever.

That thought made my stomach sink.

Finn gave a hard shove, and the platform floated gently toward the river's current. We watched in silence as her body became smaller, and smaller, disappearing with the river's flow.

The moment she was out of sight, everyone around me raised a fist, kissed their thumbs, and said, "Until we meet again."

I didn't know what to do, so I stood awkwardly, clenching my fists. Sadie didn't look at me. Instead, she spun around so fast her hair swept through the air and stormed back toward the village.

Had she been close to Penelope? They couldn't have known each other that long. I wanted to tell her how sorry I was, but I knew it wasn't the time. Sadie would talk to me when she was ready.

As people dispersed, I felt guilty. If it weren't for me, Penelope would still be here. She'd risked her life saving me and my friends, and now she was gone.

Something warm squeezed my shoulder, and I peered up to find Finn giving me a look I didn't quite understand. He wasn't smiling or trying to comfort me, yet his eyes told me not to worry—not to stress. There was something soothing about Finn's presence, almost as if he were wise beyond his years. In a sense, his energy reminded me of Grandma's. I wondered how much he'd experienced in his lifetime.

"We will be hosting a celebration of life in honor of Penelope in an hour or so," he said. "Will you join us?"

Did I have a choice? I wasn't accustomed to being asked whether I would be attending something. In Lutum, you didn't get to make decisions—you followed orders. I appreciated being asked. It felt good.

"Yes," I said. "Of course."

A hint of a smile tightened his scruffy face. "Wonderful. I'll see you then."

He left with his people. Aside from a few crying babies and whining toddlers, everyone remained quiet. Were they paying their respects? Was this a tradition? I knew nothing about it, so I remained quiet like everyone else and followed the crowd.

It wasn't until we reached the top of the slope that people began talking once again. The sound was sudden, as if everyone had been holding their breaths. Some spoke of Penelope, while most spoke of other things that had absolutely nothing to do with her—like the school's curriculum, the prior evening's supper, or their plans for the day.

I searched the countless heads, hoping to find Sadie. Despite her coldness, she was the closest thing I had to a friend. I couldn't find her. She must have taken off. Maybe she'd entered the fighting grounds to train and to blow off some steam.

"Silver!" came a familiar voice.

Next to me appeared Lyla and her brother, Lyson. Lyla beamed at me, while Lyson remained hard-faced, observing the sky as if he were practicing mathematical equations in his mind.

"That was your first, wasn't it?" she asked.

I blinked hard. "My first?"

A sudden flash of Star's lifeless body entered my mind, and I thought of Grandma, Mother, and Echo.

"Departure Ceremony," she said.

"Oh," I mumbled. "Um, yes, it was."

"Beautiful, isn't it?" she said.

Beautiful? I remembered Penelope's torn body and how her hair had gotten stuck to her pale, crispy lips. I wasn't sure I'd describe it as beautiful.

"Departing," Lyla continued. "It's a beautiful thing. I mean think about it. Imagine leaving your body—your physical body—and getting to live without pain. Totally free. Happy. At peace."

Smiling, she pointed her small, sharp-tipped nose at the sky, then sucked in a lungful of air as if breathing in the scent of fresh strawberries.

I'd never seen anyone so happy after someone's death.

"You seem sad," she said, refocusing her attention on me.

I shook my head, then shrugged. I wasn't sure how to feel. I wasn't any good at figuring out my feelings, either. It wasn't like feelings were ever talked about in Lutum. We weren't allowed to have feelings. Our sole purpose was to produce.

"I-I don't know," I said.

"Would you cut the girl a break?" Lyson said, coming back to reality. "Not everyone has our beliefs, sis."

Lyla crinkled her nose as if she'd swallowed vinegar. "I don't understand. What else could you possibly believe in?"

Lyson nudged her. "She isn't from here, Lyla."

"But I don't get it," Lyla said. "What are you taught where you come from? How do they explain death?"

How was I supposed to answer that? We weren't taught anything about death in Lutum. The only time death was discussed was when the Elites wanted to promote eternal life. The lottery was our only chance at becoming immortal. Those who didn't earn their place in Olympus were destined to grow old, die, and rot. That was the end of it. Although I'd read about *souls*, or energy, living on past the physical realm, I'd only ever thought of it as wishful thinking—something humans had conjured up to make themselves feel better about the idea of permanent death.

"I mean, when you die, you die," I said plainly.

Lyla sucked in more air, this time, nearly choking on it. "That's absurd! Where did you hear that?"

I couldn't answer her. The information hadn't come from a specific source—it was a general belief I'd grown up attached to.

"Would you leave her alone?" Lyson said. He bent forward, sticking his head past his sister to get a good look at me. "Ignore my sister, okay? She doesn't understand that not everyone believes the same thing as her."

Lyla shoved him. "That's not the point!

When you die, you die? You're wrong!"

She huffed and stormed off, leaving me alone with Lyson, who forced a smirk and offered me a one-shouldered shrug. "She'll forget all about this in an hour or so. There's a lot of death around here. Sickness and infections, mostly."

"Like Lutum," I said, matter-of-factly.

"That's where you're from?" he said. He made his eyes go big like he didn't believe me. Either that, or he didn't want to. "That's rough. I've heard stories about that place. My mom used to say she'd send me to Lutum if I didn't do what she said."

I laughed, even though there was nothing funny about Lutum.

If anything, I was more shocked by the idea of Ortus children fearing my old home more than death.

"You think death is permanent?" he asked.

We stopped walking and stared at each other for a moment. I had to tilt my head back because he was so tall. I paused, thinking it through. Permanent death wasn't what I wanted to believe in, but I'd never been given the option to believe in anything else. Religion, as Grandma had called it, was something no one spoke of—not even her. Despite wanting to learn about it, I wasn't able to. Religious texts had been destroyed a long time ago.

"I don't know what to believe," I admitted.

He smiled down at me, his white cheeks expanding. "Beliefs are beliefs. They aren't facts, even though people act that way. As Mr. Martin once said—that's Ortus's history teacher, by the way—people are often willing to die for what they believe in, and that goes to show you how powerful the human brain is. You can convince yourself that something is a fact, even when you don't have scientific proof of it."

I froze, lost in his words. Despite having a baby face, Lyson was smarter than most adults I'd ever met. It was refreshing and made me want to spend more time with him. I got the feeling that like me, Lyson spent a lot of time reading. I admired that.

"He sounds smart," I said.

"Mr. Martin?" Lyson said. We continued walking. "Yeah, he is. You'd like him."

My heart skipped a beat. Would I attend school? Or was this reserved for the younger children? For a moment, I forgot all about Penelope, the Eye, the Daemons, and the Woodfaces. I imagined a life in which I woke up every day and attended class, filling my mind with endless knowledge.

"If you like reading," he started.

"I love reading," I blurted.

He chuckled. "Wait until you see our

library. It's underground, surrounded by concrete. Something about keeping our books safe from fire. We have thousands of books. It's my favorite place in all of Ortus."

"Oh!" I said. "I can't wait to see it."

He smirked again, revealing a snaggletooth that gave him extra charm. "Come on. The celebration is starting soon."

We returned to the courtyard, where everyone gathered around the village statue. People came out of their homes carrying lit white candles. Near the statue came a group of older men with long black hair carrying skin drums. They placed them down and began positioning them in a half-moon fashion.

Lyson leaned into me, following my gaze. "Those are drums," he said. "They'll play soon. They're pretty impressive."

I was eager to hear drums. I'd never heard anyone play an instrument before.

One by one, people walked up to the statue and placed their candles next to the figure's bare feet.

"Do I need a candle?" I asked.

Lyson shook his head. "If you want to, but it isn't necessary."

We stood silently as more people gathered, including Finn, who joined us with Reina at his side. Some people cried, but for the most part, everyone seemed happy, as if this were just another day.

They stood quietly as the musicians set up their drums.

"This is new to you," Finn finally said.

I wasn't sure if he was making a statement or asking me a question, so I looked up at him.

"A Celebration of Life," he said.

I nodded.

"I imagine it's confusing having grown up with different beliefs."

How did he know about my beliefs? Was he from Lutum? Or, had he learned everything from previous Breeders?

"Sadie told us about the attack," he said. "Are you all right?"

"I'm okay," I said.

Reina clenched her fists. "That should have never happened. Silver, I'm so sorry—"

Finn raised a hand to silence her. "It's okay, Reina. You couldn't have known."

She seemed ashamed for having put my life at risk. I was surprised that Finn was so calm about it.

"What happened out there should have never happened," he said. "But if it ever happens again, I want you to be prepared."

I wasn't sure where he was going with this, but Reina nodded as if she agreed with his thoughts.

"Effective tomorrow, you begin training,"

he said.

I parted my lips, but nothing came out.

"Of course, it's your decision," he added.

I thought of the Elites, the Woodfaces, the Daemons, and how badly I wanted to fight back.

"We can't push you into anything you don't want—"

"I want to," I said at once.

Reina's lips pulled up on one side.

CHAPTER 11

I tossed and turned all night, replaying Penelope's Celebration of Life in my mind. I listened to Ortus's beating drums and the countless people chanting as they danced around the fire. The sun had set, yet people kept on dancing and singing as if time were irrelevant.

I turned over in my firm bed, smiling at the vivid memory. I remembered wishing I didn't want the celebration to end.

"Get up."

The fire, the drums, the dancing—they all dissipated and I found myself lying still inside Darby's home—my new home—with a figure looming over me. It wasn't Darby. That woman was thin and frail in comparison to this person.

I rubbed at my irritated eyes and sat up to find Sadie staring down at me with flat eyelids. "Take your time."

I opened my mouth to say something, but

my dry lips stuck together. I licked at them, trying to get the taste of dehydration out of my mouth.

"Get dressed," Sadie ordered. "We start early."

I peered through Darby's small, shuttered windows. I couldn't see any light. What time was it? Even with her shutters closed, small streaks of light crept in during the day. But now, all I saw was blackness. Was it still nighttime?

Sadie stomped her way toward the front door, her heavy boots sounding like blocks of wood being dropped on the floor.

"You'll wake—" I hissed, but Darby's voice cut me off.

"Don't you worry about me, silly. I'm always up when the sun sleeps."

She leaned back into her three-legged wooden chair and monitored the ceramic cup that sat on a strange metal contraption over a candle's flame. What was she doing? Boiling water? When she caught me looking, she said, "Would you like some tea?"

"She doesn't have time for tea," Sadie said coldly. "If you aren't outside in five minutes, you can forget your training."

I rushed out of bed and changed into the fresh new clothes Darby had set aside for me. It wasn't much—beige cotton or hemp that felt slightly rough against my fingers—but it was far better than walking around in Breeder attire and a thousand times better than the torn and stained clothes we were given in Lutum.

I rushed out while still trying to tie a knot in the rope around my waistband. Without it, I feared my pants might fall off. But I didn't mind having to wear a belt. I enjoyed loose-fitting clothes.

Sadie gave me a full up-and-down look the moment I stepped out with torn suede shoes.

"You'll need to get some boots," she said.

"I don't have any."

"We'll give you some," she said, sticking her nose in the air.

I blinked hard at the starlit sky. On the horizon, beyond the fields, a dark orange hue slowly crept its way into the sky. The sun would rise soon, and I prayed it would hurry up. Despite my long-sleeved shirt, I shivered in the morning cold.

As we walked toward the fighting area and through the damp morning grass, my shoes became wet and cold. I didn't understand why we had to start so early. I hadn't even eaten anything yet. And why was Sadie the one to wake me up?

"Are you training me?" I asked.

She grumbled something, but I couldn't

make it out. I jogged to catch up with her. "And why do we start so early? Couldn't we wait for the sun to rise?"

In Lutum, no one ever left their homes while the sun was down, so this was new to me.

"Discipline," she said sharply. "That's why. Now stop asking questions and start running."

"What?" I said.

"You heard me. Start running."

I gaped toward the open and empty field. We were the only ones out here, which made me think Sadie was only trying to torture me.

"Three laps," she ordered.

"Laps?" I said.

She sighed and rolled her eyes. "Run around the field three times."

This was absurd. Why would anyone run such a distance at this time? What was the point?

She grabbed at her hips and shifted her weight onto one leg. "Reina assigned me to train you, which means you have to do what I tell you. And right now, I want you to get your cardio in."

Cardio. What was cardio?

"Now!" she shouted.

I knew if I wanted to keep receiving training, I'd have to do what Sadie told me. Grinding my teeth, I turned away and started jogging. By my second lap, my ribs were killing me and a cramp spread out into my abdomen, making every step painful.

"Keep going!" she shouted as I slowed down.

I fought to catch my breath, my lungs feeling like they might burst into flames inside my rib cage. Why would anyone put themselves through this sort of torment? What was the point?

I managed to finish the second lap, but as I reached the end, I almost threw up. I stopped, bent forward, and rested my palms against my knees.

"Can't finish?" she asked.

Barely able to breathe, I shook my head.

"If you ever get kicked off your horse in the middle of a field during battle, how do you expect to run away from your enemies? You'd be killed in no time."

Drool slipped over my lips, dangling toward the ground.

I spat it out.

"Here." Sadie stuck a water bladder in front of me.

I grabbed it and chugged its contents, then thanked her through a series of loud gasps.

"You run every morning for the next few weeks," she said. "It won't be easy. You'll be sore, tired, and cranky, but your body will thank you in the long run. You'll adjust. That's what exercise is for. Now, finish your third lap. You can walk."

I was too out of breath to argue, so I walked, my fiery legs trembling with every step. Had I ever run before? I thought back to when I was a child, trying to play with Grandma and Mother in the gardens. But as I grew older, running became something adults didn't do in Lutum. We weren't allowed.

At last, I finished my third lap, my stomach roiling. Weak and shaky, I thought I might collapse. In the distance, the sky lightened to a deep pinkish hue and the sun began to rise.

"Go eat breakfast," Sadie said. "And come back when you're done."

"Come... back?" I said.

She stared at me like she was prepared to cut me down with words if I so much as tried to argue. "That's what I said."

"Will I be"—I sucked in more air—"running again?"

She gave me her unimpressed, flat-lidded look and turned away. What was her problem? She treated me like I was some annoying child. Why did she hate me so much?

Holding back a grumble, I marched back to the village statue, my wet shoes making sticking sounds with every step. Eventually, I'd figure out what Sadie's problem was.

As the sun rose, people gathered around

Arahm's large fire. He threw fine powder into it and his children laughed as the flames expanded twice their size.

People worked together to drag large wooden tables to the area. From the other side of the village came a dozen middle-aged men and women carrying baskets full of fruit and fresh eggs. Did they work in the agriculture area? Judging by their brown fingernails, I was willing to bet they did.

Arahm thanked them as they handed him the ingredients, then went on to set up his cooking station with the help of his children: countless cast iron pans and pots and large wooden utensils.

People continued to gather, some sipping on hot tea or coffee they had probably made inside their homes, as Darby did every day. I waited silently, watching Arahm crack eggs and cut up fruit.

When he caught me staring, he smiled, his facial hair moving with his expanding cheeks. "Are you a fan of cookin', little lady?"

I looked behind me, thinking he must surely be talking to someone else. Aside from Lyla and Lyson, no one in Ortus had bothered trying to talk to me. It was like they were too intimidated. Either that, or they didn't know what to say.

"Um, a bit," I said.

Although I knew nothing about cooking, I'd always stood next to Grandma when she made her dishes. She'd once told me that cooking was one of life's greatest pleasures, and that in a place like Lutum, she'd take whatever pleasures she could get.

"I teach a special cookin' class once a month if you're ever interested."

He smirked at me, and for the first time since arriving in Ortus, I didn't feel like a total outcast.

I smiled back. "I'd very much like that."

"Hey, Silver," came a familiar voice.

I spun around to find the two blond-haired twins standing in what appeared to be robes. They both looked exhausted, their eyes sunken like they'd spent all night playing games or something. Lyla sipped on a steaming beverage inside a white ceramic mug.

"Do you guys make those?" I asked, pointing at her mug.

She cocked a brow, pulled the mug up to eye level, and pointed at it. "This? The mug?"

I nodded and she laughed.

"No, we have tons of these lying around in our supply area. They were collected over the years from abandoned areas outside of Ortus. But some people do make their own with clay." She pointed her chin at the growing crowd, or more specifically, at the brown clay mugs a few people held.

"Do you guys go out to gather supplies?" I asked as she took another sip of her drink.

"Not much these days," Lyson cut in. "They used to, you know, when we were younger. But we have pretty much everything we need here now."

I thought back to the history books I'd read and the stories Grandma had told me. Apparently, countless abandoned houses and structures were still erect around the world. Grandma had once told me of lone survivors who lived in the vast, lifeless wastelands. But for the most part, no person ventured into these areas. Those who did often managed to find abandoned supplies.

Lyson stuck his nose in the air. "Smell that? Freshly cooked egg." He rubbed at his belly. "My favorite."

I breathed in and my stomach growled.

"Have you been assigned a job yet?" Lyla asked.

"A job?" I repeated.

She and her brother exchanged an amused look. "You might not get paid money for the work you do, but living in Ortus is payment enough. People here *want* to work, you know? I can't imagine not contributing."

"Paid?" I repeated. "Money? No, I wasn't expecting—"

"She's messing with you," Lyson said. "It's a joke in poor taste." He nudged his sister. "Everyone in Ortus knows that slaves—I mean, *people* from Lutum—don't get paid for their work."

I didn't respond. It had definitely been in poor taste.

"Why are you all sweaty?" Lyla pointed out.

Not only was I sweaty, but it felt like my cheeks were on fire. I wondered if they were as red as they felt. Probably.

"Morning run," I said. "I'm being trained."

Lyson threw his head back. "Ahh, so that's your job."

"What is?" I asked. "Training?"

"Yeah," he said. "You're being trained to become a Champion, or something in that department. Beatrice Hawthorne—Ortus's Counselor—works with everyone to make sure they're happy with what they do. But I bet someone higher up wanted you to be a Champion, so you got to skip the whole counseling part. Probably because of your reputation. Lyla here works in the daycare, and I manage the library."

My jaw dropped. "You *manage* the library? You didn't tell me that."

He smirked charmingly. "I like the element of surprise."

Lyla's eyes darted between her brother and

me. "Okay, well when you two are done flirting, I'll be getting my breakfast over here."

Lyson forced a laugh. "I'm not—hey, get back here." He rushed after his sister.

As he ran after Lyla, the space around me got quiet. Too quiet. It was almost as if all sound had been sucked out of the air. What was going on? Was someone staring at me again? Or, had I lost my hearing?

Heads turned in unison toward the western side of the village, where three figures slowly walked out from within the darkness.

Dax.

Danika.

Rose.

They walked with their shoulders slouched and their eyes cast toward the dirt floor. Danika pulled her red hair over one shoulder like she was trying to hide her face from the crowd. Dax, being much taller and more muscular than her, had nowhere to hide. It wasn't like Dax to look fearful. She'd always been the strong and silent type. Rose seemed to take advantage of Dax's build. She walked behind her, trying to hide from everyone in the village.

"Dax!" I shouted, my voice the only sound in the entire village. "Danika," I said more quietly. "Rose." I rushed toward them and they met me with relieved gazes.

"Silver," Danika said. She threw her arms around my shoulders.

Dax gave me a nod of acknowledgment, but I ignored her discomfort for affection and hugged her tight. Next, I reached for Rose, who didn't hesitate to hug me back. When I pulled away, I searched their faces, their shoulders, their bellies.

"Are you guys okay? Are you hurt?"

The three of them shook their heads at the same time.

"Only a few bruises and cuts, but nothing serious," Danika said. "Rose has the worst of it." She pointed at Rose's dark arm, where a gash ran from her elbow to her wrist. It must have been a deep gash, because they'd stitched her up.

Although Rose never spoke, she gave me a sweet smile that I knew meant, *I'm okay.*

Dax ran a hand through her short, curly brown hair. "How are they treating you here, Silver? Are you okay? Will we be okay?"

I sighed outwardly. "Honestly, yeah. This place feels like heaven. I mean, aside from the training I'm going through. You can make your own decisions here."

"Training?" Dax said.

I fanned my face, still trying to cool off from my morning jog. "Yeah. I'm going to be a Champion."

She searched the people behind me, her brown eyes narrowing into slits. "A Champion? What's that?"

"A fighter," I clarified. "To defend Ortus. To fight back against our enemies. Against the Elites."

At the sound of Elites, she stiffened and her jaw muscles popped. "How do I sign up?"

"Back there." I pointed toward the stable area, where I'd seen a lineup of recruits the day prior. Finn had told me they were all signing up to be Champions, which meant anyone could join.

She bashed a fist into her palm. "Awesome. Thanks."

Danika, on the other hand, didn't seem all that interested in the violence. She played with her hair again and smiled as children ran around their parents, kicking a suede ball about the size of a soccer ball.

"What will you do?" I asked Danika.

Jolting out of her trance, she said, "Huh?"

"What do you want to do here? My new friends over there said everyone gets assigned a job. Some lady named Beatrice will probably talk to you at some point."

Danika stared off again, admiring the children's laughter.

I glanced down at her belly, though it didn't look large. "Are you pregnant?"

With slanting eyebrows, she shook her head. "No, but I wish I'd found this place before I gave birth to my little girl last month."

I reached for her shoulder. "I'm so sorry, Danika. I can't even imagine."

She nodded fast and wiped tears from her eyes.

Rose smiled up at her, then quietly leaned her head on her shoulder.

I wondered how many babies Dax and Rose had lost. I didn't ask. Instead, I kept quiet, waiting for Arahm to finish cooking breakfast. When he was done, he whistled and called me up first.

"To our new guests!" he shouted, prepping three plates of eggs, cantaloupe, and grapes.

Everyone clapped as we approached, and I felt more uncomfortable than ever.

I thanked him and his children, then led my friends away from the common grounds and toward the fighting grounds. Between the two areas was a path that ran from the cavern entrance all the way to the agriculture area. It was quiet here, so I brought them underneath a lilac tree where we sat on boulders.

We ate in silence for a while until I couldn't hold it in anymore.

"Can I ask what they looked like?" I said.

Both Danika and Dax froze with food in their ballooned cheeks.

"The Daemons," I said. "No one is giving me a straight answer, and since you've seen them—"

Dax swallowed her cooked egg. "Like monsters."

"I wouldn't say monsters," Danika said. "I mean, yeah, it was really messed up, but they're human, if that's what you're asking."

I stared at her, wanting more.

"They're severely deformed," she continued. "There were about five or six of them."

"Seven," Dax corrected.

"Seven," Danika continued. "They wore bloody animal pelts, had crazy hair that looked like it hadn't been cleaned or brushed their entire lives. One of them only had one eye. The other socket was hollow. Another had two noses that took up half of its face. Most of them had more than ten fingers, and they all had overly long nails and rotting teeth."

Despite being human, they sounded like monsters. No wonder Lyla and Lyson had said as much.

Danika stared into nothingness, no doubt remembering the horrendous day. "They almost looked like—"

"Like what?" I pressed.

"Like experiments," she said. "Like someone altered them genetically."

She and Dax exchanged another look, one that told me they'd already discussed theories.

"What is it?" I asked.

Dax took a bite of a cantaloupe and licked her wet lips. "Well, you said they kicked us out of Olympus because some doctor figured out how to make babies, right?"

"Yeah," I said.

"What if all those years leading up to their success, they made a bunch of mistakes?" she said.

"Mistakes?" I repeated. "Like babies coming out wrong?"

"Exactly," Danika said. "It makes sense. Look at how easily they threw us away. It isn't so far-fetched to think that they created messed-up experiments and threw them out, too."

Mutated babies? Scientific failures? It added up, almost too perfectly. I felt sick to my stomach.

CHAPTER 12

"Y"ou can do better than that," Sadie said.

She watched me with a carelessness that made me wonder if she even wanted me to succeed as a Champion. Every time I threw my spear, she gave me a look that said, *You'll never make it.*

I wasn't doing well. My ribs still hurt, making it difficult for me to throw as hard as I wanted to. She'd positioned me at the far back of the field, away from everyone else, and told me to hit a giant wooden target against the mountain wall.

Unfortunately, no matter how close I got, I kept missing.

At one point, the spear hit the target, but it did so on an angle and bounced off rather than going through the wood. Sadie then proceeded to show me how it was done. With legs parted and her back stiff, she fired the spear as if it weighed nothing more than straw. It spun through the air at lightning speed before stabbing right at the center of the target's red circle.

It made me feel small and weak, but at the same time, it inspired me to keep practicing. Maybe one day, I'd become as good as Sadie.

After about twenty-some throws, my shoulder started to ache. I rolled it back, wincing in pain.

"Don't tell me you're already sore," she said.

I glared at her. "I am. What do you expect? I've never thrown a spear before, and my ribs are still hurting."

"Tough luck," she said. "Whining won't get you anywhere with me."

"I-I'm not whining!" I said. "I'm hurting. There's a difference."

"Fight through it," she said.

Gritting my teeth, I threw my spear into the grass. "What's your problem? If you hate training others so much, why are you training me?"

Sadie planted her hands on her hips and took a step toward me. "I didn't ask for this. Reina did. She wanted me to be the one to train you."

"Why?" I said. "Clearly, this isn't your thing. You're a horrible teacher."

"And you're a horrible student," she said. "But I had no choice. It was Reina's orders."

I threw my hands in the air. There was no getting through to her. She was only doing this because Reina had forced her to. She didn't want to teach me. She didn't want to be anywhere near me.

"I can't throw anymore," I said. "I'm done."

I stormed away with Sadie calling after me. "We aren't finished!"

But I didn't care. I was done. My shoulder was burning beyond belief, making it harder and harder to throw the damn thing. Why bother continuing? I'd only keep missing my target, and Sadie would only keep making fun of me. Maybe after I rested for a bit, I'd come back.

I left the fighting grounds as several heads turned my way. Many people held on to bows, swords, and fighting sticks, and some even froze midfight to watch me leave. I hoped Reina wouldn't see me, but I was afraid that if I didn't walk away now, I might say something I regretted.

I needed to cool off.

When I entered my new home, Darby lay in her bed in the corner of the room, facing the wall. I stared at her gray hair, wondering if being allergic to the sun made her miserable. She didn't seem to mind. Besides, she'd probably lived most of her life like this, so she was accustomed to it.

Careful not to make any noise, I removed my damp shoes and made my way over to my bed, wincing in pain. Right when I lay down, a faint knock on the front door made me jolt back up.

I shot a look in Darby's direction, hoping it hadn't woken her. When she didn't budge, I got up and tiptoed my way to the door. Who would it be? Sadie? Had she come to apologize for being such a pain?

I hoped so.

With my left cheek against the wall, I creaked the door open. To my surprise, Sadie wasn't the one standing outside—it was Reina.

She stared at me with a look I couldn't quite make out. Was she upset with me for having left the grounds? It didn't look like it. If anything, she seemed concerned.

I cleared my throat. "R-Reina."

"Silver," she said straightforwardly. She peered into the darkness behind me. "Do you have a moment?"

I glanced back at Darby who was still sleeping, then stepped outside with my bare feet. The earth was cool against the soles of my feet, but it felt good.

"I saw you leave your training session," she said.

I stared at her weapons belt and the metallic sword dangling on her right side. It was intimidating, to say the least.

"Y-yeah," I said. "I'm sorry. I'm hurting pretty badly."

She cocked a brow as if I'd told her I had levitating abilities.

"Training can be hard on the body, but I don't think that's why you left."

Reina was more insightful than I gave her credit for. What did she want me to say? That I couldn't stand Sadie? That she was being a total jerk about training me? I didn't want to insult Sadie or make her look bad to her superior.

"Sadie can be a handful," Reina said as if reading my mind.

I searched her eyes, waiting.

"I know she comes across as angry and hateful," she continued, "but I assure you, she's your best match. One of my best Champions."

I parted my lips to say something along the lines of, *Well, she doesn't want to train me*, but I closed my mouth.

Reina smiled knowingly and turned away, making her way toward the path separating the village from the fighting grounds. Although she didn't ask me to follow, I got the feeling I was meant to. So I walked next to her as we crossed a patch of lush green grass and climbed onto the dirt path.

The sun was brighter now, and voices

carried throughout Ortus. Everyone was out and about, doing their jobs or tending to their responsibilities, and here I was, pouting. It made me feel ashamed.

"The thing you need to understand about Sadie is that she's been through a lot."

I listened carefully, watching my bare toes as I walked.

"She told me about the attack." She paused and glanced sideways at me as if trying to determine whether I had suffered psychological trauma from that event.

"Yeah," I said. "Woodfaces. She didn't seem to like them very much."

Reina forced a laugh and searched the clouds, her sculpted jawline looking even sharper. "That's one way of putting it. Our treaty with the Woodfaces is fairly new. It was Finn's way of putting a stop to an impending war."

We moved away from the houses and started walking near the garden beds, where countless people moved about like working ants, tending to plants of all different shapes and sizes. One woman leaned so far into her garden bed to reach for green beans that she almost tipped over.

"A while back, I led a mission outside of Ortus to gather supplies. There are a few abandoned towns near here, one of which at the time still had a few valuable resources: kitchen supplies, clothing, weapons. What I didn't know was that the Woodfaces were also scavenging the area that day. The moment we arrived, they attacked. Moira, Sadie's girlfriend, was on the front lines when the attack started." She paused and stopped walking, likely reliving that awful day. "A dozen arrows came down on her. She never stood a chance."

I wanted to say something, but I wasn't sure what, so I remained silent.

"Sadie lost her love that day, and a few days later, the treaty was signed, so she also lost her chance at ever avenging her."

I couldn't even imagine how much hurt Sadie must have felt. I'd asked to become a Champion because I wanted to stand up to the Elites to avenge my Grandma and my mother. But Sadie? She'd been forced to make peace with the very people who'd taken her love away.

"Sadie has a lot of anger to deal with, especially when it comes to making new friends."

"What do you mean?" I asked.

Reina placed her hands on her weapons belt and stared off toward Ortus's wooden barrier. "She doesn't want to get close to anyone. I don't blame her. Many lives are lost in Ortus. We don't have an advanced medical facility like Olympus has."

"But I thought you celebrated death," I said.

She let out a laugh through her nose. "That's a lot easier to do when it isn't someone close to you. There's still pain, even if you know they're in a better place. There's still the realization that you will never see that person again. At least, not in this lifetime."

I averted my gaze, afraid I might start bawling at the thought of Grandma.

"I-I'm sorry," Reina said. "I imagine you've lost people as well."

Clenching my jaw, I nodded. It took everything in me not to drop to my knees.

We stood in silence for a moment, until Reina turned around. "Sadie's waiting for you," she said. "Come on."

CHAPTER 13

The next few days played out as I expected them to.

Sadie continued being her usual cold self. But knowing it was a defense mechanism made it more tolerable. I reminded myself that she was hurting inside, and she was doing everything she could to push me away.

Every morning, I woke up with crusted eyes from having cried myself to sleep thinking about Grandma the night before. I also woke up sore, which helped distract my mind.

Push through it, I told myself.

It wasn't until the fourth day of training that I became so sore, I found it difficult to get out of bed. Fortunately, just as I opened the front door, a wave of relief washed over me.

It was pouring outside.

I thanked whoever sat above the clouds for giving me a day off. Although Sadie had tried to warn me that there was no such thing as days off, I'd also heard through other people that heavy rain meant everyone got to stay inside. She'd only said it to discourage me.

I was about to close the door again when Lyson came running toward me with a wool blanket over his head. He winced as the water drenched the fabric, but it didn't slow him down.

I opened the door and urged him inside.

"Thanks," he breathed. "Wow, it's nasty out there."

"I don't mind," I admitted.

"Here." He handed me a book wrapped in a leather binder.

"What's this?" I asked.

"Something for you to do," he said. "Since this is your first rainy day, I figured you weren't prepared."

I peeled away the wet leather and peeked inside.

The Lion, the Witch and the Wardrobe, by C. S. Lewis.

I smiled. "What's this?"

He seemed as excited as me. "A really good book. I think you'll like it."

"Thank you, Lyson. This is great."

He kept staring at me as if expecting me to say something else. When it became awkward, he cleared his throat, put the wool fabric over his head again, and said, "Well, I'm heading back. I hope you have a great day." He reached for the handle, then turned his head to the side. "Oh, and in case you're wondering, breakfast and supper are served at each door on days like this. Arahm has a cart with a roof that he pushes around, so expect a knock."

I couldn't help but smile. Food delivery? I was beginning to feel like royalty.

I beamed, clutched my new book to my chest, and thanked him again as he left with a smile.

As I jumped back into bed, excited to dive into a world of limitless possibilities, Darby sat up and yawned.

"Oh, I hope I didn't wake you—" I said.

"No, no, don't be silly. I have a strange schedule."

She got up and went into the small bathroom—a room no larger than a closet with a flimsy wooden door. I slipped under my sheet, cozied up against my pillow, and started reading.

I got so entranced by my new book that I jumped when a knock echoed from the front door. Darby waved her wrinkly hand at me, urging me to stay put, and collected our breakfast from cheerful Arahm. He made jokes and laughed as he handed Darby fluffy-looking honeycombs from his sheltered cart.

When the door closed, the mouthwatering

warm smell of something sweet swept through the air, making it nearly impossible to focus on my book.

"Well?" Darby said, placing the plate down onto our small kitchenette table. "Don't you want a bite?"

My stomach growling, I lurched out of bed and joined her as she spread maple syrup across the golden cakes.

"Fresh from Ortus," she said.

"The maple syrup?"

She smiled, her cheeks ballooning on both sides. "Well, all of it, I suppose. The wheat, the eggs. But yes, I meant the syrup."

The *wheat*? What were those things, anyways? I stared at the golden honeycombs in my plate.

Darby smiled sweetly. "Waffles. A bit like pancakes, but different. You'll see."

I sat down, grabbed a fork, and dug into one of the crispy, golden honeycombs. The second it fell onto my tongue, I rolled my eyes, thinking my head might explode.

Darby laughed. "Good?"

"I can't... Wow. I mean..." I tried, savoring every second of it.

Darby rolled her shoulders back proudly. "We sure do make good syrup here."

I blotted my sticky lips with a white cloth next to my plate. "I've only eaten maple syrup once before. We didn't have any in Lutum. And this—" I pointed my fork at the waffles. "Wow."

Darby's bright blue eyes tripled in size as if I'd just told her that spiders had invisible wings.

"How unfortunate," she said. "Why is that?"

I shrugged. "Tastes too good, I bet. The only other time I tasted maple syrup was in Olympus."

She stared at me as if physically aching over my words. Then, without warning, she laid a cold hand over mine. "Life is short," she said. "Make the best of the one you have."

We ate in silence for a while until Darby finished her plate and set her fork aside.

"Silver," she said, matter-of-factly. "May I ask you something?"

For a moment, I hesitated. She stared at me with such intensity that I wondered if maybe I'd done something wrong. Maybe she no longer wanted me as a houseguest.

I nodded slowly.

"Why did you refuse?" she asked.

I wasn't sure what she meant by this, but I must have scrunched my nose. She squeezed my hand and added, "Immortality."

Was the rest of the village wondering the same thing? Did they gossip about it? No one dared ask me, though. Instead, they all watched me when they thought I wasn't looking, likely playing a guessing game among themselves.

"I didn't want to leave my family," I said.

As the words came out, I immediately felt stupid. If I hadn't refused immortality, Mother and Grandma would still be alive, along with countless innocent people who were slaughtered because of me.

"It appears difficult for you to talk about it," Darby said.

I cleared my throat, willing my tears away. "Yeah, it is."

She smirked and moved her red bulbous nose close to me. "Can I let you in on a little secret?"

I nodded. I wanted to talk about anything other than me.

"I would have done the same thing," she said.

This took me by surprise. Every time people heard about what I'd done—refused to receive the immortality serum—they looked at me like I was crazy. It was like they couldn't understand how anyone in their right mind would reject eternal life.

"This is borrowed," Darby said, pulling at the thin, stretchy skin on her forearm. When she let go, it took a while to bounce back into its original position. "Our bodies, they aren't *ours*. They're only shells. What you did was noble. If someone offered me eternal life, I'd tell them to shove it." She paused and stiffened her posture. "I'd tell them, no thank you. I'm plenty happy to die and be free."

"Really?" I asked, my mouth agape.

"Absolutely," she said. "The most beautiful thing about life is getting to experience it through different phases: as a child, a teenager, an adult, and even an old person." She laughed and pointed at her gray hair. "I can't imagine living on this horrible planet for all of eternity. It isn't natural. Flowers die. Grass dies. Everything dies. And then, there's new life."

"I-I never thought of it that way," I admitted.

Darby tapped her veiny temple. "Dying is like a badge of honor. It means I lived my life. I made it. To not die, well, I'd get bored. And lonely. Nature shouldn't be messed with like that."

She let go of my hand and pulled away. "Your reason is even better than mine."

"What do you mean?"

She smirked. "I would refuse eternal life simply because it isn't natural. I want to live a natural life. You, on the other hand, rejected it for love. For family. That's something, and I bet that's why people are willing to follow you anywhere. Even if they don't yet know the truth. They can sense you're a good person. I could."

"Follow me?" I jerked my head back. "I don't even know where I'm going."

Darby parted her lips to add something else, but a loud knock interrupted our conversation. I urged her to stay seated and opened the front door.

Sadie.

What was she doing here?

"The rain's slowing down," she said. "Meet me at the grounds in ten minutes."

I craned my neck and searched the gray, overcast sky. Although it wasn't pouring anymore, it was sprinkling—enough to get Sadie's hair all wet and frizzy. A few droplets of water sat still at the tip of her nose, glistening.

"Do I have something on my face?" she asked.

"What? No," I said. "Won't the ground be all wet?"

She crossed her arms and glared at me, making my knees buckle. "I'm sorry, do you control the weather?"

What was she talking about? I opened my mouth, but she cut me off to continue, "Oh my God. I didn't know that Silver Morewood was a goddess. Wow." She fanned her wet, shimmering face. "I had no idea she could clear the sky during battle. So maybe the next time we're out there and it starts pouring, you can make it all go away. You can make the ground dry again and control our environment to give us the advantage—so we can fight like we train here in Ortus. On dry grass, with a clear sky."

By the end of her outburst, her fake, overstretched smile was gone and she scowled at me.

I made my eyelids go flat. Someone was in a mood.

"I'll be out in a few minutes," I said.

Without a word, she turned away and left.

The second I closed the door, Darby started laughing—a cute, high-pitched chuckle that made it impossible not to smile. But I didn't understand what she found funny. Sadie had been an absolute nightmare.

I gawked at Darby and waited for the laughing to stop.

"She's a firecracker," Darby said. "But you should admire that. You really should. Sadie is probably the only person in all of Ortus with enough guts to talk to you like that."

I scoffed. "And why would I admire that? She treats me like garbage. Others may not talk to me, but at least they're polite and respectful about it."

Darby placed my plate over hers and began clearing the table. "Being polite and respectful to one's face doesn't mean anything, Silver. People talk. Many are making assumptions about your life. Sadie, on the other hand, is the type of person who isn't shy about asking questions if she wants answers. Isn't that better? Besides, you're quiet, reserved, and new to the outside world. I think Sadie is good for you."

I wasn't sure how to respond, so I thanked her for cleaning my plate and left.

CHAPTER 14

"*G**ood for me*," I grumbled all the way to the fighting grounds.

I didn't see how someone like Sadie was good for me. She made me nauseous with those intimidating eyes of hers and turned my cheeks flaming hot when she scolded me. She made me uncomfortable in every sense of the word.

On what planet was that good for me?

As I walked across Ortus's main path and up toward the fighting grounds, I sensed something was different today. Everything was quiet. Had Sadie ordered me back on the grounds knowing no one else would be there? It was only drizzling out, so I imagined others would be training, too.

I rounded the wooden fence but stopped when I spotted hundreds of Champions lined in rows at the field's entrance. They stood tall with arms at their sides, gazes fixated straight ahead as Reina paced back and forth on a black horse.

Something hard suddenly smashed me in the shoulder and Sadie walked right past me. She snapped her head sideways. "Are you coming, or what?"

I followed her to the group and we joined the side rank.

A few eyes followed our movements, but no one moved. Champions stood like wooden toy soldiers lined up on the floor.

"Some of you may have heard the rumors by now," Reina shouted over the light rain. "We were attacked during a mission a few days ago."

Whispers broke out among the Champions and a few heads turned to look at Sadie and me.

"These attacks were brought on by the Woodfaces."

Gasps filled the open field and a few frightened faces swept from side to side.

"Woodfaces?" someone shouted. "I thought—"

Reina shot the man a fierce gaze and he immediately stopped talking. It was obvious that she enforced order and obedience. No one else spoke out as she pulled on the reins of her horse and came back to our side, bouncing lightly on her saddle.

"This morning, we sent a messenger out to

renegotiate the terms of our treaty with the clan's leader," Reina continued.

Next to me, Sadie clenched her jaw, her muscles popping out with every bite. I wanted to tell her how sorry I was to hear they were still trying to negotiate with killers, but it wasn't my place. Sadie didn't even know that I knew about her past. Besides, I'd also just learned that speaking while Reina was giving a speech was a sure way to get in trouble. So I stood quietly and listened.

"We will await their response," Reina shouted, "but I want you all to be prepared. Train hard, sharpen your weapons, and practice your aim. If things don't go as we hope, we will have no other choice but to go to war."

A heavy silence weighed down on everyone. It was one thing to fantasize about fighting our enemies, but it was quite another to hear that the possibility was very real—to know that any day, we might be forced to go out and fight to the death.

"You are dismissed," Reina said.

Chatter broke out instantly, with some people making it obvious how displeased they were with the idea of a second treaty.

"This is ridiculous," someone said. "Why would Finn give those savages a second chance? They almost killed Tray."

"Maybe to avoid more casualties," someone responded.

"The only way to avoid casualties, in the long run, is to eliminate the threat. They broke our treaty!" someone else shouted.

Sadie stormed off and marched toward our usual training area at the far back of the field. I chased after her, barely able to keep up with her long strides. The last four days of brutal exercise had almost wrecked me.

I chased after her. "Hey! You okay?"

Sadie craned her neck and laughed aloud toward the clouds. "Okay? Am I okay? Those savages nearly killed us. They have no right to be given a second chance."

I was surprised she hadn't said a word during Reina's speech. She respected her leader enough to keep her mouth shut. I parted my lips to agree with her when the sound of trotting hooves approached us.

Sadie ignored Reina as she approached and instead, grabbed her spear from out of the grass. "Let's just train."

"Sadie," Reina said.

Sadie whipped her spear at the target, cracking the wood.

"Sadie," Reina repeated, a bit louder this time.

Sadie was fuming—that much was clear. I imagined that she avoided eye contact with

Reina for a reason. Maybe if she allowed herself to look at her, she'd lash out. Reina sighed through her nose and climbed off her horse.

She waited in silence as Sadie walked briskly toward the target to rip her spear out. When she came back, she stared at the grass, rather than at Reina.

"Soldier," Reina said, more coldly this time.

Sadie stopped walking, planted the end of her spear next to her boot, and looked up at Reina. She seemed annoyed about it.

"Sadie, this wasn't my order," Reina said. "You have to understand—"

"Understand?" Sadie hissed.

I blinked hard as she stormed toward Reina. "What is there to understand? Those fucking savages deserve to be dead, and yet we keep giving them chances."

"Watch your tone," Reina ordered.

Sadie's throat bulged as she swallowed and looked away. I couldn't tell if she wanted to punch someone's face in or burst out crying. Her right eyebrow twitched, and she kept swallowing hard.

"I agree that by breaking our treaty, they deserve retribution," Reina said. She was shorter than Sadie, but this didn't take away from her commanding presence. She took a step forward and planted two hands on her leather weapons belt. "Finn doesn't want more lives lost if this can be discussed civilly."

"Right," Sadie said. "Because having dozens of fire arrows shot at us was civil."

"I'm not here to explain their actions," Reina said. "I'm here to tell you that this is political, and it's beyond my control. What have I always taught you?"

Sadie kept quiet.

Reina lowered her head, trying to catch Sadie's gaze. "Well?"

"To fight with my head and not my heart," Sadie said.

Reina nodded. "Now, as your friend, I'm asking you to set your emotions aside and focus on training. If you can't do that, we'll need to reconsider your position."

Sadie breathed in loudly through her nostrils, then out through her mouth. It took her a few seconds to look at Reina again, but when she did, she seemed like a different person.

"Okay," she finally said.

Okay? How had she let go of all her anger so suddenly? I wanted to ask her, but I kept my mouth shut.

"Good," Reina said. She climbed back on her horse and trotted away.

The second Reina was gone, Sadie pointed her chin out. "Pick up your spear. Let's keep practicing."

I did as she directed.

After a dozen throws, I asked, "Seriously. Are you okay?"

She hesitated. "What do you care?"

I pulled my face back. I wasn't sure whether to defend myself or try to comfort her. "I may not know you very well," I said, "but I still care if you're hurting inside."

"Why?" she said. "That's stupid. You should mind your own business."

"You're the closest thing I have to a friend here in Ortus," I said.

First, her eyes went big as if I'd just slapped her across the face. But then, her brows came together and it became obvious to me that she didn't want me referring to her as my *friend*.

"We aren't friends," she said coldly. "Besides, I could never be friends with someone like you."

I jabbed the end of my spear in the grass and took a step toward her. "What's that supposed to mean?"

She laughed, though it didn't sound genuine. "Oh, please. You're a legend, Silver, don't you know? Not only did you get all of your people killed, but you also got your friends kicked out of Olympus and tossed out of a train. Why on Earth would anyone want to be friends with you?"

I gritted my teeth, trying to remind myself

153

that Sadie didn't know what she was talking about. She was good at what she did—at poking and prodding to take the attention away from her.

"I didn't get my people killed," I said slowly, scowling up at her. "They stood up for themselves to fight the injustices of Lutum. You wouldn't understand that, though. You grew up living a life of luxury here in Ortus. You don't understand what it's like to be a slave. What it's like to have no rights and to be beaten when you speak out—"

"Silver—" she tried, likely wanting to take back a few of her words.

"No!" I shouted, pointing a stiff finger at her. "You don't get to treat me like shit and accuse me of being responsible for taking countless innocent lives. I didn't kill anyone. The Elites did. They're the enemies. They're monsters. And here you are, acting exactly like them. Blaming me for something *they* did. Blaming the victim. I lost my mother, and my grandmother at the hands of the Elites." My throat swelled, but I kept going. "You think this is easy for me? You think I like being a *legend*? I hate it! Everyone is talking about me, and I don't know what they're saying. Some people think I'm some hero, and others hate me. I didn't ask for any of this. All I wanted was a quiet life with my family, even if that meant

154

living a life of slavery. Even *that* was taken away from me."

"Silver—"

"And you make it sound as if I got my friends kicked out of paradise. Do you even know what goes on in Olympus? Or do they keep that from you here, too? To *protect* you? Me and my friends were called Breeders, and Breeders only serve one purpose—to produce children for the Elites by getting inseminated against our will every month."

Her jaw went slack.

"For your information, I didn't get my friends kicked out of Olympus. That was going to happen anyway the second Dr. Bartek figured out how to grow babies in a lab—"

Sadie's eyes widened. "What? What are you talking about? What babies?"

I grabbed my hips and breathed hard, trying to catch my breath. "The Elites can't reproduce," I said. "It has to do with the serum. It messes up their reproductive systems."

"So they host annual lotteries to pick fertile women?" Sadie said.

The confused look on her face told me that the people of Ortus didn't know much about Lutum, or about the Elites. I wondered if Finn and the other high-ranking authority figures like Reina kept details secret to protect them from harm.

"Yeah," I said. "That's exactly what they do. And now that they've figured out how to make their own babies, they don't need the people of Lutum for that. Don't you see how dangerous that is? They're going to expand their kingdom until it's big enough for them to be self-sufficient. And when that happens, they won't need the people of Lutum anymore. They'll slaughter them all."

"Silver, I had no idea—"

She reached for me, but I yanked away and clenched the handle of my spear. With all of my anger, I threw it as hard as I could into the target, piercing the red center dot and splitting the target in half.

CHAPTER 15

"That was one hell of a shot," came Dax's voice.

I tore my spear out of my broken target.

"You okay?" she asked.

I inhaled a deep breath, willing my negative emotions away. It wasn't Sadie's fault that she didn't know the whole truth about Olympus. I supposed what hurt was that she was so up front about everything else, so why hadn't she simply asked me? Why had she made such awful assumptions about me?

And why did I care so much?

"What are you doing here?" I asked, my tone coming out a bit colder than I'd hoped.

Dax shouldered her wooden bow and raised an arrow. "I signed up." She turned on her heels and pointed at a young man with light brown skin, a beard, and long black hair fastened in a bun. He stood near the archery range, drinking from a water bladder.

"That's Pete," she said. "He's my new trainer."

I watched as a dozen people fired arrows at their targets. Why had Sadie put me on spear throwing? The way I saw it, firing arrows was way more practical. Quivers carried several arrows, whereas spears, well, you only had one shot.

"Is that your trainer?" Dax asked, slyly shifting her gaze to Sadie.

When Sadie caught us looking, she turned away and left. I wondered if I'd upset her with my outburst.

Even as she walked away, Dax kept staring.

"Yeah," I said. "She's something."

"I agree," Dax said.

Why was she watching her like that? Like a hungry hyena eyeballing a piece of meat?

"What are you doing?" I asked.

Dax's lips pulled up on one side. "Nothing, yet."

"What are you talking about?"

"Come on," she said. "Look at her. She's drop-dead gorgeous."

"What's your point—" But I stopped myself, realizing where this was going. "You're attracted to her."

Dax looked at me like I wasn't a total moron. "Who wouldn't be?"

I watched Sadie as she left the field, looking

as small as a toy figure from this distance.

"You do know she's the devil, don't you?" I asked.

Dax burst out laughing, a huge smile splitting her square face. She rubbed at her dimpled chin and said, "The hardest shells usually have the best tasting interiors."

I wasn't sure whether to smack her or to tell her to leave. Something about the way she'd looked at Sadie annoyed me. She wasn't a piece of meat. I'd seen other guys look at Sadie that way, especially when we were together, and it bothered me every time. It was an unnecessarily long gaze that made me uncomfortable.

"Pete's waiting. I'll catch you later." She smacked my shoulder and jogged toward the other archers.

Alone in the field's corner, I figured it was a good time to continue practicing. I made my way back to the target area, removed the broken target, and hung up a new one. About a dozen wooden targets lay in a pile on the grass, which meant this sort of thing happened often. I certainly wasn't Hercules.

I managed to land another dozen shots before Sadie came back with two water bladders. Without a word, she handed me one, and I drank from it. It was cold and fresh and I nearly drank the whole thing.

Wiping my wet lips, I thanked her and placed the bladder down into the grass.

We didn't talk for the next few hours. It was uncomfortable, but it was better than being insulted for having a lousy throw. I supposed it was becoming impossible for her to insult me since I was starting to land most of my shots.

"You're getting good," she said.

I appreciated the compliment, but I didn't say anything. I wanted to, but I couldn't.

After nearly cracking the second target, I turned around and asked, "Why did you train me on spears? Why not archery?"

Sadie looked over her shoulder and at the archers firing arrows into their targets. "Spear throwing takes a certain physical control that not everyone can master. It builds muscles. It teaches you to use your body in a disciplined way rather than relying on a wooden structure to keep your weapon straight."

"Will I learn to use a bow?" I asked.

She shrugged as if I were asking for something as plain as water. "Yeah, tomorrow."

We kept training until the sun began to set and the village loudened with an evening crowd. In the distance came an orange glow—no doubt Arahm's cooking fire—that made my stomach growl.

With aching shoulders, I walked quietly next to Sadie as we left the field with other

Champions. My back was killing me, and while I would have preferred to learn how to shoot arrows, I was thankful for Sadie's unconventional methods. I was probably one of the only ones in the field, aside from Sadie, capable of throwing a spear dead center of its target.

Everyone else seemed preoccupied learning how to use a bow, a sword, or fighting sticks. While I wanted to learn all of those, it would take time, and I was thankful to Reina for having assigned one of her best Champions to be my trainer, even if we didn't always see eye to eye.

I parted my lips, about to thank her for today's training session, when a scream echoed near Ortus's cavern entrance. Rapid footsteps stomped on the ground as people gathered, wide-eyed and confused.

I shot Sadie a glance, but neither of us needed to say anything to know what to do next. We bolted side by side toward the scream. Near the entrance stood Reina and Jayun, trying to get a hold of a frantic horse neighing and standing on its rear legs.

But it wasn't the horse's erratic behavior that caught my attention—it was its empty saddle and the blood splattered across its white and beige coat. There was so much of it that at first, I'd thought the horse to be brown.

It tore its long face away from Reina's grasp and ran off, nearly stomping over a child. The father managed to pull his little girl away in time, and the horse took off toward the garden beds. From the stables, Maz came running out, waving a scarred arm above her head. She whistled, then made a clicking sound with her teeth, but the horse couldn't hear her.

In a haste, she jumped on another horse with such ease it looked like she'd levitated, then kicked its sides and chased after the runaway.

"What's going on?" Sadie asked.

Several other Champions and citizens had gathered, but Reina urged them to keep their distance.

"Give us space," she ordered.

She didn't say the same to Sadie, though. It was almost as if she trusted Sadie enough for her to overhear what was happening. What kind of relationship did they have? Was Sadie her second-in-command?

Everyone else backed away while we stood next to Jayun, who rubbed at his bloodstained face.

"Where is he?" Reina asked.

"The entrance," Jayun said.

Reina took a firm step forward, prepared to enter the cavern when Jayun's dark, muscular arm stopped her.

"No," he said. "It's best you don't see him."

"What happened?" Sadie asked. "Where's Roland?"

I assumed Roland was the messenger Reina had sent out earlier that morning—the one who'd been asked to discuss the terms of our treaty with the Woodfaces.

Jayun shook his head solemnly. It was clear that whatever had happened to Roland was too gruesome for any of us to see.

"Decapitated," Jayun said.

Reina flattened her palms against her temples and turned away to catch her breath.

When she spun back around, Jayun handed her a leather envelope.

"What's this?" Her dark eyes searched his.

"Their terms," Jayun said.

As Reina opened the envelope, Finn came racing toward us on his horse. He stopped suddenly, dirt and dust forming a cloud around our legs, and jumped off.

"What happened?" he asked.

Reina's nostrils flared as she finished reading the letter inside the envelope. I wanted so badly to know what it said, but it wasn't my place to ask. In the distance, everyone watched us, waiting to hear the news.

Reina handed the letter to Finn, who read it carefully, his jaw muscles popping every few seconds.

Reina stood silently as he read. It was as if she were afraid to make eye contact with anyone—if she did, she could inadvertently reveal what she knew.

Finn breathed out hard and searched the sky as if the clouds held the answers he needed. Then, he looked back down at Reina. "Why are they doing this?"

With her hands still on her hips, she shook her head as a way of saying, *I don't know.*

"Doing what?" Sadie asked.

Reina pointed at both of us and said, "You're dismissed."

Sadie glared at her. "We have a right—"

"That's an order," Reina said.

Sadie sealed her lips and balled her fists as if wanting to punch a tree.

When she turned away, Finn said, "No, it's okay. They have a right to know."

"Are you sure?" Reina asked.

He nodded slowly, inspecting the faraway crowd. It was as if he wanted to ensure that only we hear the truth. He forced a smile, raised a hand, and shouted, "We have this handled. Please, enjoy your supper and we will make an announcement as soon as we know more."

Reluctantly, people withdrew back into the village, near Arahm's fire. In the distance, Maz returned with the runaway horse fastened to hers by a rope. She led it back toward the stables and disappeared inside.

"The Woodfaces have rejected our offer to discuss terms," Finn said, his voice directed at me.

Why was he talking to me?

"Their violent response proves that they have no intention of negotiating terms." He sighed and rubbed his palms together. "Instead, they've made a demand."

"A demand?" I asked. "What do they want?"

He stared at me a bit longer than necessary and his jaw muscles bulged again. "You."

CHAPTER 16

Sadie's home was cleaner than I would have expected.

She was always in such a bad mood that I pictured her home looking messy. But everything in here was dust-free and shiny as if she spent every evening scrubbing a different corner.

I toured around the small space, admiring her wooden furniture. Next to the front door was a small kitchenette table that looked much smoother and shinier than Darby's, which made me wonder if she received special privileges for being a Champion.

Did common citizens receive unfinished furniture, while Champions had access to better quality? Next to Sadie's bed was another little nightstand with the same dark orange finish. It sparkled under the natural light streaming in through her small windows.

Curious, I ran my finger along the smooth

varnish.

"Don't touch that," she ordered.

I pulled my hand away as if I'd been caught trying to plant flowers in Lutum.

"I-I'm sorry," she said. "Moira made those for me."

I turned to her. I knew Moira was her girlfriend—the one she'd lost a few years ago. But Reina had told me this in confidence, so I figured it was best not to open my mouth about it.

Instead, I said nothing, and Sadie eyed me curiously.

"Aren't you going to ask me who that is?" she said.

"I, um," I stammered.

She smiled for the first time and my heart skipped a beat.

"I'm not an idiot, Silver. Your demeanor toward me completely changed after your little outburst the other day. That means you know about my past, which means someone told you."

I didn't know what to say. I didn't want to mention Reina's name—the two of them were seemingly close, and the last thing I wanted was to make her feel betrayed.

"You're a terrible liar," she added.

Was she insulting me?

Again, a weak smile tugged at her lips. "I

hate liars, so I guess that's a good thing you can't lie to me."

I forced a smile, my lips tightening unnaturally. I wasn't sure how to behave around her. One second she was cold and downright rude, and the next, she showed me an ounce of humanity that made me question her sanity. I'd never met anyone like her before.

She pointed at her bed. "You can sleep there tonight."

I spun around a few times. There was only one bed. "What about you?"

She shrugged. "I can sleep on the floor."

"You know, I can go back—"

"No, it's fine," she cut me off.

I wasn't even sure why I'd asked to stay with her the night. I could have easily returned to my home with Darby and gone to sleep. But after what happened—after learning that the Woodfaces wanted me—the only person I wanted to be around was Sadie. She made me feel safe.

"How about you stay here, and I'll get us supper?" she asked.

I didn't object.

She left through the front door and returned soon after with two plates of lentils and vegetables. I thanked her and we ate in silence. For the first time, it wasn't awkward. I didn't feel the need to open my mouth to break the silence.

I was too preoccupied thinking about the days to come. Would I even be alive tomorrow? Would Finn send me away to save his people? It was the right choice, after all. Why go to war when a single sacrifice could end it all? Sadie had made it clear to me that Finn made choices to protect his people, even if it meant making sacrifices.

We didn't talk for the remainder of the evening. I lay in bed, pulling the thin sheet up to my neck as my heart raced against my ribs. Would they hang me? Decapitate me? Gut me? The jumble of thoughts made me nauseous, so I rolled over and stared at the wall, trying to think about anything else.

I must have tossed and turned for hours as Sadie lay quietly on the floor next to me.

After several dozen leg jerks, her voice took me by surprise. "Can't sleep?"

"Did I wake you? I–I'm sorry—"

"No, you didn't," she said. "It takes me hours to fall asleep."

I rolled onto my back and gazed up at the dark, dome-shaped ceiling.

"You think Finn will hand me over?" I asked.

The sound of lips unsticking echoed beside me, but she didn't say anything. Was she afraid to answer? Did she already know the truth?

"I don't know." After a beat, she added, "I

hope not."

Hope not?

Those were the nicest words Sadie had ever said to me. It made me feel warm and comforted despite my terrifying circumstances.

"Hey, Sadie?" I said.

"Yeah?"

"I'm sorry for yelling at you earlier."

She let out a forced laugh through her nose. "I deserved it."

"No, you didn't," I said. "I was a jerk."

She laughed again, and although I didn't know what she was laughing at, I couldn't help but join in. We laughed and laughed, until finally, things got quiet and she said, "I've been a bitch."

"What does that mean?" I said.

She laughed even harder. "I guess you aren't taught swear words in Lutum."

I thought back to when I was young, and how Grandma had always told me to keep my mouth clean. She said dirty words were a way of releasing intense emotion and the Elites had no tolerance for it. I knew a few basic words, but only those I'd read about.

"Not really," I said.

"What about fuck?" she asked.

I bit my lip. "I've heard it, but I don't really know what it means."

She laughed again. "It means a lot of things. Probably one of the most versatile words in the English dictionary. It can be a noun, an exclamation, and a verb."

I rolled to my side to face her. "Does the library have a dictionary?"

I heard her lips crack into a smile. "That's what you're thinking about right now? You're excited about whether or not Ortus has a dictionary available?"

It sounded silly now that I thought about it. Tomorrow, I could be dead, but the thought of getting to read through an actual dictionary kept me smiling.

That, and Sadie's laughter.

"Hey, Sadie?" I said.

"Yeah?"

"Can we start archery tomorrow?"

She paused, almost as if she were fighting with herself to ignore reality. I knew that by morning, I may be put on a horse and sent off to the Woodfaces. But it was easier to pretend that wasn't real—to imagine a world in which I continued training with Sadie, eating delicious suppers every night and going to sleep soundly.

After a moment of silence, she said, "Yeah, whatever. If that's what you want, princess."

I beamed into the darkness, closed my eyes, and went to sleep.

I woke up with a jolt, grabbing my chest to feel my heart beating against my palm.

I was here, alive. I hadn't been kidnapped in my sleep and sent away. The smell of fresh-baked muffins wafted through the air, making me want to sit up solely to follow the scent.

"Morning," Sadie said.

She sat at the table, watching me with her piercing blue eyes as she bit through what looked like a blueberry muffin. Bits of bread crumbled down her forearm and onto the table. "Brought you one."

"I slept through breakfast?" I asked.

She nodded and slid the muffin across the table toward me. "I let you sleep in. Don't get used to it. It was a one-time thing."

I was thankful for the extra few hours. I got up, my aching body making me wonder if I'd stepped into a time machine only to come out fifty years later.

I grabbed the muffin, admiring its mushroom-like shape, and twirled it around a few times. It made me think of Rolie and how he'd brought me a cupcake on my birthday. I hadn't gotten to eat it since Mother had thrown it on the ground.

"How did they make this?" I asked. I squished it on both sides, making the top move up and down. It was like bread—something I was awfully familiar with from my Lutum days—only much softer and greasier.

Sadie stopped chewing midbite and stared at me like I'd tripped and hit my head. "An oven."

"I thought Arahm cooked over the fire."

"Not always," she said. "Haven't you ever been inside the community center? Some people go there when it rains. There's a kitchen and everything."

My stomach sank. What if this was my last day? I hadn't even seen the library yet. And now, Sadie spoke about a community center.

"Do you want to see it?" she asked.

My eyes shot up at her. "See what?"

"The community center."

I lit up. "More than anything."

She finished her muffin, nodded with her cheeks ballooned, and wiped her hands over the table, sending bits of muffin everywhere. "All right. Eat up."

I finished eating my blueberry muffin, even though I didn't want it to end. Every bite made me drool. It was the most delicious thing I'd ever tasted. Was this what cake tasted like? It almost felt wrong, like something this delicious shouldn't be eaten for breakfast.

Once I finished my breakfast, Sadie gathered both of our crumbs, bunched them into her fist, and threw them out the window.

I hurried and got dressed, removing my pajama top and slipping into my daily Champion uniform—a green hemp T-shirt with matching pants. I washed it every evening with soap and a bucket of cold water, and left it to hang inside. When it was nice out and we weren't expecting rain, I hung it outside. Everyone did this.

In Lutum, we were only allowed to wash our clothes once a week to conserve water.

Being that Ortus sat next to a river, we had no limitations, which ensured everyone—for the most part—smelled fresh most of the time.

Sadie led me out of her home and toward the main path. But when we stepped on, someone whistled. I glanced up to spot Reina standing next to a horse with its reins in her palm. She pointed at us both and then toward the training grounds.

What was going on?

I hoped Sadie would argue on my behalf. But she didn't.

"Where are you going?" Reina asked.

Sadie stiffened and straightened her arms. "I wanted to take Silver to see the community center, ma'am."

Reina's gaze narrowed at the rising sun. "You're already late, and now you want to go play around at the community center?"

Her voice became harsh, and I felt guilty, like I was the one responsible for getting Sadie in trouble.

"Ma'am," Sadie tried.

Reina raised a finger, ordering her to keep her mouth shut. "We don't have time to be fooling around, Sadie. This isn't a joke. I want Silver trained on every weapon by the end of the day, and I want her to start riding."

Sadie knit her brows, looking as confused as I felt. Why was she acting like this? As if yesterday hadn't happened? We were all there. We knew exactly what the Woodfaces had demanded, and couldn't very well go on about our day acting like nothing had changed.

"But Reina," she began, sounding much more casual this time around, "Silver deserves—"

"I don't want to hear another word," Reina said. "We go to war in three days, and you'd better be ready."

CHAPTER 17

Keep your elbows up," Sadie said, readjusting my stance.

I punched at the padded gloves she wore, knocking them back.

"That's it," she said.

After what felt like a hundred punches, I wanted to lie in the grass and take a nap. So I dropped to the ground, and although I didn't take a nap, I lay motionless for a few minutes, watching the birds overhead. I was beyond exhausted. But Sadie kept pushing me—kept telling me that we were limited on time, and if I wanted to survive what was coming, I needed to train as hard as I could.

I'd tried arguing with her. The way I saw it, if I trained too hard, by the time things got real, I'd be too exhausted to fight. But Sadie wasn't having it. So I obeyed every order and learned as much as I could from her.

"All right, let's move to riding," she said,

likely noticing my sweat-stained shirt.

Breathing hard, I tried to calm my aching lungs and nodded.

She offered me a hand, so I took it and she yanked me back up onto my feet. I followed her to the stables where she introduced me to Carrot—the training horse. What I found most amusing about Carrot was that she had a white patch between her eyes that resembled a carrot with leaves, especially in contrast with her brown coat. When I pointed it out, Sadie laughed at me and said, "She's obsessed with carrots. That's how she got her name."

I shrugged and wiggled a finger at Carrot's face. "Still looks like a carrot to me."

Sadie led Carrot out into the field, near other riders who were practicing jumps and sharp turns.

"Carrot is one of the most docile and patient horses we have," Sadie said. "She won't kick you off, and she won't get spooked, so don't be scared."

Although I'd never admit it, I *was* scared. Carrot was huge. I'd ridden on the back of a horse a few days prior, but I hadn't been the one in control. What if I messed up? What if I gave the wrong command and Carrot took off running at full speed?

No doubt sensing how tense I was, Sadie patted my shoulder. "Relax, would you?"

I inhaled deeply through my nose and breathed out through my mouth.

"It takes time to learn how to properly ride a horse," she said, fastening a saddle on Carrot's back. She attached the reins around her head, and Carrot didn't seem to mind at all. She stood quietly, letting it all happen.

Once the gear was fastened, Sadie climbed up and explained everything from how to sit properly, to using your feet to make the horse run at different speeds. I made her repeat herself a few times to make sure I understood everything, but even then, it was overwhelming.

She climbed down. "All right. Your turn."

"What?" I sputtered. "I'm not ready. What if I—"

"Relax," she said. "I'll be holding on the whole time. We'll start slow."

And we did.

I sat with trembling legs as she guided the horse by a lead. I swayed back and forth every few seconds, carrying most of my weight against the feet slots on either side of the saddle. It made me feel more secure. It also helped that she'd given me a pair of leather boots as promised—she said that when riding, it was crucial to have the proper equipment.

We walked around the field twice, and by the end of our second lap, I felt a bit more at ease on the majestic beast.

"Good girl," I said awkwardly, patting Carrot's soft, warm neck.

Sadie smiled, and I found it hard to look away from her. When she caught me staring, she cleared her throat. "Okay, time to try a lap on your own."

"What? Not yet—"

"You'll be fine," she said. "If you want to stop, use the reins and pull back. Eventually, you'll learn to do this with your body, but Carrot knows the drill. And whatever you do, don't squeeze your legs or kick at her sides. I want to see a walk—not a trot or a canter—just plain walking."

With eyes bulging, I gripped the reins. My heart pounded hard, but in a sense, I liked it. I was terrified and excited at the same time. For the first time in my life, I was about to ride a horse.

Oh, if only Grandma could see me doing this.

Sadie moved back, leaving me alone with Carrot.

"Whenever you're ready, give your calves a good squeeze on either side of her belly. Don't squeeze again at any point—"

I squeezed and Carrot started moving.

I spun around to see Sadie getting smaller as Carrot led me down the side of the field.

"Whoa, this is really happening," I said,

grinning from ear to ear.

"Go, Silver, go!"

I snapped my head sideways to spot Dax waving her bow over her head, making me smile even more. This was incredible. A few other people started cheering and I laughed. As Sadie had taught me, I used the reins to guide Carrot around the bends and made my way to the other side of the field.

As I came back, I spotted Finn entering the field. He made his way over to Reina near the stables.

What was he doing here? Did he have more news on the Woodfaces? Although tempted to squeeze my legs again to move faster, I didn't. Sadie had warned me against doing anything rash. Slow and steady, she'd said.

So I slowly rode toward the stables, wanting to jump off the horse and run to Finn. By the time I returned to Sadie, Finn had turned around and was exiting the field.

"That was great," Sadie said.

I pulled on the reins to stop and climbed down clumsily, nearly toppling over.

"Silver," she began.

"Finn!" I shouted, running toward him.

"Silver!" Sadie hissed.

Clearly, yelling after the leader of Ortus wasn't something people were supposed to do around here. Even Reina gave me a disapproving look as I ran past her. But I didn't care. I needed to know the truth. Why hadn't he sent me off to the Woodfaces, as they had demanded?

When I approached, he rubbed his beard and watched me with curious eyes. "Silver," he said. "Can I help you with something?"

Panting, I jogged up to him. "What's going on? Why am I still here? Why haven't you—"

"Silver," he said in a manner that told me I ought to be careful with my next words. "How about we discuss in private?"

"Private?" I said. I followed his gaze over my head and realized that several people were watching, likely wondering what someone like me wanted to say to the leader of Ortus.

He led me back toward the stables, and the moment we entered inside the solid wooden structure, Maz rose from a kneeled position next to a horse's hoof. She wiped dirt from her knees, bowed courteously at the two of us, and walked out.

I stood quietly, breathing in the scent of horse manure and hay.

"Why am I still here?" I asked.

He led me farther toward the back of the stables where shovels and rakes hung on a metal rack.

"Silver, you have to be careful," he said, his voice sounding like shards of glass. "People don't know about that letter or about that threat."

"And you're keeping it from them," I said, feeling somewhat irritated.

I thought the leader of Ortus was different, that Finn was honest with his people, unlike the Elites with theirs.

"The situation is complicated," he said.

I wasn't buying it.

"How is it complicated? Don't get me wrong, I'm happy that you haven't sent me to the Woodfaces, but I don't understand. Why would you risk the lives of all your people to save mine?"

He breathed in slowly as if weighing his answer. "The world isn't black and white, Silver. There are gray areas. This, unfortunately, is a gray area."

I wasn't sure what he meant. He turned away and began pacing, his leather boots stomping over dirt and hay.

"The last thing I want to do is go to war." He rubbed his forehead as if it would somehow help him think. "But the Elites will never stop enslaving people and ruining the lives of innocents. We need to look at the big picture. Your presence here is igniting fires within people. You bring about a desire in people, Silver. A need to stand up to the injustices of this world. A desire to fight back."

"Why do you think the Woodfaces want me?" I asked.

He stopped pacing and crossed his arms, lost in thought. "I don't know. I haven't yet figured that one out. But I do know that if we hope to ever win against the Elites, we need you. My people need you. Battle isn't what I want—"

A scream suddenly pulled our attention away. I peered out through the stable's open barn doors and into the vast field, where countless Champions gathered, craning their necks to look at something up above.

I ran out and searched the clouds.

Oh no.

I'd hoped I'd never see that machine again.

It hovered with a gentle sway as if suspended by an invisible wire. It released a soft humming sound, but nothing loud enough to draw attention, especially over voices. Someone must have spotted it.

"What is that?" someone cried.

From the village came more voices. Although I couldn't see the crowd forming from here, I imagined countless adults surrounded by children, pointing upward with mouths agape. The children were probably laughing, wondering what kind of animal could fly without wings.

"The Eye," I breathed.

"Everyone inside!" Finn shouted.

His voice came out harsh and strong, making me flinch. At once, panic spread like wildfire. People ran away from the fighting grounds and into the village, their heavy footsteps sending vibrations up my legs.

Reina ran toward us, her eyes unusually wide. "How did it get here? I thought we were safe, between the mountains."

Finn glared toward the flying machine. "I don't know."

He parted his lips, then sealed his mouth. It was apparent he had no idea how to handle the situation. This whole time, he must have thought, or at least hoped, that he and his people were safe so long as they remained within the confines of the mountains.

Yet somehow, the Eye had found us.

I blinked hard as it drew in closer, its black lens focused on me. It made a buzzing noise as it descended a few more feet, clicking and popping. What was it doing? Taking pictures?

Finn stepped in front of me like a protective parent. "Get inside, now."

I walked backward into the stable, my stomach sinking. The Eye hadn't been looking for Ortus; it had been searching for me.

CHAPTER 18

My heart raced as people ran in a panic, trying to hide from the Eye's view.

Reina rode in circles on her horse, urging people to get out of the fighting grounds. It amazed me how well she rode, capable of taking sharp turns as if the horse were an extension of her own body. As people ran from left to right, exiting the field, I spotted Sadie rushing against the traffic.

What was she doing? Why wasn't she leaving? I considered running out after her, but with the way the Eye was focused on me, I wondered if it was waiting to fire some sort of weaponry.

Was it *that* advanced? Did it have some high-tech laser capable of obliterating me where I stood?

Sadie bounced around as shoulders slammed into her, her hair getting tangled in her face, but she didn't seem to care. She was looking for something, and it was obvious she wouldn't stop searching until she found it.

Suddenly, she grabbed a young girl by the collar of her shirt and tore a finely carved spear right out of her hands. With slits for eyes, she leaned back, aiming the spear's point at the back of the Eye.

With all her might, she thrust the spear into the sky.

The point penetrated the device instantly, causing sparks to fly in every direction. The Eye made a strange intermittent buzzing sound before its swaying became erratic. It flew from side to side, up and down, as if either unaware of its location or simply too dazed to coordinate its movements.

Everyone froze, watching the black-and-white device twitch a few more times before descending to the ground at full speed.

"Watch out!" Reina shouted.

Most people had already cleared the area, and those remaining jumped out of the way just in time.

The Eye landed hard in the grass, right in front of the stables. It buzzed, releasing a static sound unlike anything I'd heard before.

Sadie marched up to the device despite Reina telling her to stay back, planted her boot on its metallic frame, and tore her spear out. Several red and white wires followed, dangling lifelessly over the Eye's large black lens.

Slowly, I stepped out of the stables, cautiously approaching the alien equipment. Everyone else moved as slowly and formed a crescent moon around the collapsed Eye.

"Nice shot," Dax said.

She offered Sadie a sly smile, but Sadie didn't acknowledge her. She was too busy staring at me.

"You okay?" Sadie asked.

I nodded, moving toward her. "Is it dead?"

The Eye sparked one last time before all sound left its body.

"Think so," Sadie said. "Looks like a drone."

I'd never heard the term *drone* before.

As more bodies crowded the lifeless piece of machinery—or the *drone*—the air became thick and loud. People asked all sorts of impossible questions, calling out, "Where did that come from?" and "What does it want?"

Finn and Reina looked at each other as if exchanging telepathic messages. Did they know more than they let on?

Finn approached the shiny machine and knelt on one knee. He ran his finger along its black glass lens and across the slick white metal of its body. What was he searching for? Some sort of imprint? His finger stopped on something and he looked up at Reina.

She moved toward him with a hunch in her

back, slowly lowering herself to his level.

"Ambrosia Inc.," she read softly. "What is that?"

He gave her a meaningful look that told me we were all in grave danger.

"The Elites," he said.

Several people gasped and others stepped back as if the machine would blow up any second. Could it still see us? Hear us?

"What does it want?" Reina asked. "We've never done anything to the Elites."

Finn sighed and looked at me over his shoulder. He went on to mumble something else to Reina, but it was difficult to hear with everyone panicking. People pointed at the Eye and started bickering about its origin and its intention.

I knew what it wanted and so did Sadie: it wanted me. *They* wanted me. First, the Woodfaces had demanded I submit to them, and now, the Eye showed up. I was wanted. I wasn't sure if the two groups were connected, but it didn't matter. My being here was putting everyone in danger.

I gritted my teeth. I was growing tired of the Elites. Not only had they killed my people, and my family, but now they were coming after me and my new friends. I wished they would all die.

I thought back to the young children inside

Olympus's courtyard and immediately felt guilty. They weren't all responsible—especially the children. They were born and raised inside Olympus without knowing right from wrong.

Ambrosia. Why did that sound so familiar?

"What's Ambrosia?" I asked, leaning into Sadie. "What does it mean? Finn seems to know what it is."

Sadie shrugged. "Finn knows stuff."

How did Finn know so much about the Elites?

"You look confused," Sadie said. "Do you need me to spell anything out for you?"

I wasn't in the mood for her smug comments. I waved a hand as a way of telling her to keep her mouth shut, but all she did was laugh.

"You're so transparent," she said.

This pulled my attention away from Finn and onto Sadie. What was that supposed to mean?

"It's like I can see your brain twirling from here." She poked my forehead. I went to swat her finger away, but she was too fast.

"What are you talking about?" I said.

"You're trying to figure it out." She turned slightly, pointing her chin at Finn who stood with his arms crossed, talking to Reina. "You're trying to figure out how the leader of Ortus knows so much about the Elites. Are you worried he's an enemy? That he's going to betray us?"

Her last questions came at me almost in a mocking tone, as if the very idea of Finn betraying his people were more ludicrous than the idea of pigs flying. Was it, though? People could never be trusted.

"I'm surprised you don't know by now," she said.

I scowled at her. "Know what?"

She paused, holding on to the information long enough to torture me. It was like she was enjoying watching me squirm. Finally, she smirked. "Finn's an Elite."

I stared at Grandma with wide eyes, trying to read her lips. Maybe if I paid closer attention to the way her lips moved, and the way her tongue flicked her teeth as she spoke, I'd understand what she was telling me. But it didn't make sense.

"You're twelve now," she said, stroking the side of my cheek with her thumb. "You should know these things."

"But I don't understand how it works. Can you explain it again?"

She smiled sweetly at me, the folds in her cheeks deepening. "Elites are immortal. Well, they don't age. It doesn't mean they can't die."

"So, if they get sick, they could die," I said.

"Or injured, yes," Grandma clarified. "But the injection they're given alters their genetic makeup. It basically stops the process of aging, but it doesn't reverse it. I wish I had more information for you, sweetheart, but I'm not a scientist. I don't know how it works on a molecular level. All I know is that the Ambrosia Project was initiated by a group of people who wanted to live forever—people who didn't want to age. And now, they live in Olympus and are in charge."

"So that's what the lottery is for," I said, not really expecting an answer. "To give people the chance at getting the injection."

Grandma rubbed my cheek again and smiled. "Exactly. If you're chosen, Silver, *you* could become an Elite."

"That's impossible." I gritted my teeth and took a step toward Finn, but Sadie grabbed my wrist.

"Relax," she said, pulling me back. "Being an Elite doesn't make someone evil. It only means he was raised in Olympus."

I tore my hand out of her grip and glowered at her. *Didn't it make him evil?* Wasn't he one of them?

She laughed at my anger. "See? This is why Finn waits to tell newcomers *what* he is. Believe it or not, Silver, Finn is an innocent in all of this, too."

"Innocent?" I sneered. "How? He's immortal, like the rest of those monsters. Why should we follow someone who grew up living a life of luxury in Olympus?"

For the first time since I'd gotten to Ortus, I looked at Finn with animosity. I felt he wasn't genuine. How could he have kept something so big from me? Was I overreacting? Or was everyone else underreacting?

Sadie sighed and watched Finn from a distance. "You two aren't so different."

I was about to scoff when she added, "He was the first Elite to successfully run away from Olympus."

Successfully? What did she mean? Had others tried and failed? And why would anyone run away from a life in Olympus? Despite how cruel they were to the people of Lutum, they took care of their own. He'd likely grown up never wanting for anything.

"It was decades ago," she said. "Him, his wife, and his daughter. They ran, hoping to build a new life for themselves, away from Olympus. He doesn't talk about it much, but he compares Olympus to a prison. There are comforts, but there is no freedom. He also felt sick at the thought of Lutum slaves supporting his daily living. To everyone here, he's a hero."

I didn't say anything. I couldn't. How had I not known?

"Where's his wife?" I asked. "And his daughter?"

Sadie sighed again. "Unfortunately, they were caught."

"Caught?" I said. "What do you mean?"

She stared at the grass, and then at her toes. "Finn doesn't know what happened to them. He waited by the tracks for months, but they were never thrown out of the train."

"Are they dead?" I asked.

Sadie shrugged. "I don't know. No one knows. Finn has been trying to think of a way to get them back for years. He's been working hard, building an army to stand up to the Elites, but it's a slow process. Ortus wasn't built in a day. It started out with a few rogues in the wilderness and took decades to populate."

I froze, watching Finn as he turned away from Reina and approached the Eye. In sync, they bent down, picked it up, and slid the machine into a horse-drawn cart. Finn climbed onto the wooden platform, as did Reina, and ordered Maz to ride off.

He sat quietly with his legs dangling off the edge of the cart, looking defeated. Was he thinking about his wife and daughter? I couldn't imagine his pain. I thought back to his house, where I'd first met him, and remembered the sad look on his face as I admired the paintings on the wall. Many of them depicted scenes of early Ortus, when only a few houses had been built.

This whole time, Finn had no way of knowing whether his wife and child had been slaughtered, enslaved, or imprisoned. Had they been allowed to carry on their lives? Had his wife remarried? I watched him ride away, shrinking every few yards. If there was one person fit to lead Ortus, it was Finn.

We stood in silence for a while, until something gnawed at me. "You said Finn was the first one to run away successfully. Have there been others?"

"Only two others," Sadie said. "But they both died of disease. We do have a few survivors from Lutum here, though. They're older. They managed to escape Lutum years ago before the concrete walls were put up."

I stared into the village as if the survivors would magically become obvious to me.

Sadie elbowed me. "Darby's a survivor."

Darby? As in the woman I lived with? My jaw went slack. How was this possible? How young was she when she ran away? I wondered if her skin condition had had something to do with her wanting to escape.

"There are a few others in Ortus. The stories they shared with us about their lives as slaves are what sparked people to start training. That's always been Finn's plan, you know."

I locked eyes with her. "What has? War?"

She shook her head. "To free the people of Lutum."

CHAPTER 19

Gossip spread throughout all of Ortus that evening.

By nightfall, people were still talking about the Eye and making speculations about why it had entered Ortus and what it wanted. How would Finn handle this? He'd disappeared with Reina and Maz into his home and refused to come out. A few other well-respected citizens had joined them and hadn't been seen since.

Were they discussing options? Planning something? After supper, many people stayed up despite the village's habit of going to sleep along with the sun. The large village ·fire danced from side to side as people gathered with their stools, sitting side by side to discuss the day's events.

After Sadie and I finished our supper—roasted lentils and bell peppers—we walked away from the fire, sensing countless eyes on us. Did they know the Eye wanted me? Was everyone too afraid to voice it aloud?

I stared at my house, where a faint orange glow shined from the crack of the closed window. Darby was no doubt awake, sipping on tea as she did every evening. All I wanted was to go to sleep and forget the day, but I didn't want to leave Sadie's side.

Scratching the back of my neck, I hesitated. She must have sensed my thoughts.

"You want to stay with me again?" she asked.

"Y-yeah."

She led me back to her place, where we spent the next several hours lying side by side—with Sadie on the floor—talking about anything and everything. I learned that Sadie had lost her parents to a fire about a decade ago when an awful drought nearly brought Ortus to its knees. She remembered being about ten years old when it happened, and Reina had stepped in to console her and distract her from her heartache by teaching her how to fight. I now understood why she and Reina had such a close bond.

The more Sadie told me about her life, the worse I felt for having judged her. Not only had she lost her parents at a young age, but she'd lost her girlfriend of five years very recently. She spoke highly of her and commented on how witty her girlfriend had been. Any time a puzzle needed solving, Moira was there to solve it.

After her stories, Sadie went quiet, so I started telling her about my life: about Lutum, my angry mother, and Grandma, who always took care of me.

"Doesn't that infuriate you?" Sadie asked.

"What?" I said.

"That you lost your family because of the Elites."

I paused. Of course, it infuriated me.

"Because you don't show it," she said.

I smiled at the ceiling, even though there was nothing to smile about.

"Grandma always taught me that emotions are private," I said. "I guess most people in Lutum are raised that way. We aren't allowed to be angry or upset. Those who ever lashed out at the Elites or the Defenders turned to ash."

"Ash, like vampires." She laughed, but when I didn't respond, she added, "Wait, you're serious? What do you mean, *ash*?"

"The Defenders have these weird weapons that obliterate a person in a second."

"Holy shit," she mumbled. "I-I had no idea. I thought the Elites didn't kill people."

I blew out a lungful of air at the ceiling. I didn't understand it myself. But based on what the president herself had told me, I had a pretty good idea of how the Elites operated. "I think they're superstitious when it comes to taking lives on actual Olympus territory."

The sound of chafing echoed beside me, likely Sadie shaking her head. "That doesn't add up. If that were the case, they could have easily thrown you out of the train and shot an arrow through your heart."

I swallowed hard at the thought. Sadie wasn't wrong. Why was it that in some instances, the Elites could obliterate a human being, and in others, they refused to draw blood? Why go through all the trouble of casting people away on a train when they could simply obliterate them the way they did the people of Lutum?

"Maybe they don't kill anyone who's ever set foot inside of Olympus," I said.

I envisioned Sadie pensively scratching her chin.

"I guess that makes sense," she said. "Either way, those people are sick in the head."

"Most of them," I defended.

I wasn't even sure why I was defending the Elites. But I thought of Finn and his family, and then of Adryan Thompson—the Peacemaker who brought me to Lutum to deliver my speeches. He'd spoken of Olympus as if he didn't agree with their methods but was too afraid to speak out. I wondered if he'd heard of Finnigan Wren, or if anyone inside of Olympus had heard of this mysterious man who ran away and built his colony.

Did they view him as a hero? Surely, they'd heard about me. Had my story encouraged other Elites to take a stand against their leaders? I was getting ahead of myself. For all I knew, the good people only made up the smallest portion of Olympus's population. The rest were likely brainwashed or simply didn't care.

I closed my eyes, envisioning freedom for the people of Lutum, until everything went black.

The next morning wasn't anything like the other one I'd spent with Sadie. There were no blueberry muffins nor kindness on Sadie's part. Maybe she'd woken up stiff from having slept on the floor, which in turn had put her in a bad mood. Either that, or she was stressed out about how the day was going to unfold.

"Get up," she ordered.

I sat up slowly, rubbing my eyes with my knuckles. Through her partially opened window came a cool breeze.

"It's still dark out," I said.

"I didn't ask you what time of day it was, Silver," she said. "Come on. We don't have time to waste."

I got dressed and followed her to the fighting grounds. It wasn't until we entered the field that I reached for her arm, forcing her to stop marching so fast.

"What's going on? Why are you being like this?" I asked.

It was so frustrating to make progress with Sadie, only to have her revert to her cold ways. I never knew what to expect from her. One day, she managed to smile at me, and the next, she gave me death glares that made me want to drop to my knees and beg for her forgiveness.

I hated it.

Her jaw went slack, but then she paused as if holding back many lies. Finally, she let out a lungful of air. "Everything is wrong, Silver. Don't you see that? Finn has been consulting all night with Reina, Maz, and whoever else is in there."

"They probably went to sleep—"

She scoffed and pointed at Finn's house. It sat tall, above all other houses on its massive wooden posts. From behind the windows came a dim orange glow that told me no one was sleeping.

"They aren't sleeping, trust me," she said. "I've been up all night, watching."

204

"What do you think is going to happen?" I asked.

She started marching again.

"Hey, wait!" I called out, but she ignored me.

I gave up trying about halfway through the field when I realized Sadie probably hadn't the slightest idea what was going to happen—that was why she was freaking out. She couldn't control it, and Sadie liked to control things. Like Mother, it probably made her feel safe.

So I quietly trained with her for hours until the sun came up. As excited as I was to be learning to use a bow for the first time, I never thought I'd have to learn in the dark. Sadie told me this was the best way to learn—that it was easier to master something difficult and then move on to something easier.

I wasn't so sure I agreed, but I knew better than to question her methods.

So I stood with my legs at shoulder width, firing arrow after arrow, when my stomach started growling. I parted my lips, prepared to say something along the lines of, "I might be better at this if I got some food into my stomach," when a loud, heart-stopping horn echoed throughout all of Ortus.

I froze with my bow gripped, having just shot an arrow and missed my target.

"What was that?" I asked. "They don't

usually announce breakfast—"

"Not breakfast." Sadie dropped her bow and jogged down the empty field. I tossed mine on top of hers and followed her out of the grounds.

When we entered the village, Arahm and his many children were in the middle of prepping their food station. The kids prepared the fire and brought fresh foods to the table. If the horn hadn't been about breakfast, then what was it about?

Slowly, people exited their homes in a daze.

At least I wasn't the only one who was confused.

Some scratched their heads, while others wrapped themselves in warm blankets and yawned. Everyone searched the area as if trying to determine the source of the loud sound.

Within minutes, Finn came galloping toward the houses on horse. Behind him were Reina, Maz, and another man I didn't recognize. They slowly trotted past the houses and toward the village statue, careful not to crush any feet along the way. Parents pulled at their children, holding them tight against their bodies.

"Can you believe this?" came Dax's voice.

She stood next to me, her gaze focused on Sadie more than me.

"Believe what?" I said.

She glanced my way for a moment. "That big machine hovering over the village yesterday."

I supposed not everyone knew what it was called.

"The Eye," Sadie corrected.

Dax narrowed her eyes on Finn. "What do you think he's here to tell us? This can't be good. Danika says the kids are pretty freaked out."

"What kids?" I asked.

"Didn't she tell you?" Dax said.

I hadn't spoken to Danika in a few days, nor Rose, and it must have shown on my face.

"She's working in the daycare now," Dax said. "She says—"

"I apologize for the early awakening," Finn shouted. "But we have an important announcement."

I was surprised when no one gasped. Instead, everyone remained tight-lipped, clutching onto their loved ones in the chilly morning air.

Finn bowed his head, causing anticipation to build. Was this it? Would he admit to everyone that I was the reason for all of this danger? Was I even the reason? Sure, the Woodfaces had threatened the village, asking to have me handed over. But what about the

Eye? What if it wasn't related at all?

"We need to evacuate Ortus immediately."

Finn's words came out sounding deep and ominous. At once, everyone blew up into a fit of rage. Men punched the air and women shouted, "This is ridiculous!" and "What about our children? This is their home!"

Finn raised a palm and everyone went quiet. "I understand why you're all upset. I truly do. This isn't easy for me. We spent years building this village from the ground up. But I assure you that this is our safest option. We have already been attacked by the Woodfaces—"

"The Woodfaces?" shouted a man with long hair over his shoulders. He was tall and overly muscular, as if he spent his days lifting small horses. He stepped forward, in front of his wife and young son. "When were we attacked? Was it the other day? That was them? Everyone saw it, Finn. The blood, all of it. We heard a man was decapitated."

A few mothers slapped their hands over their children's ears and gave the man a venomous look.

By all of it, did he also mean the part about Finn reading the note? The one in which the Woodfaces demanded I be given to them?

Finn nodded. "That was them."

Gasps filled the village, but Finn raised his

hand again and the cries stopped.

"We are facing threats from the Woodfaces," he continued, "and now, the Elites."

"The Elites?" said the same long-haired man. "But how—"

"The machine some of you saw in the sky," Finn said, "it belongs to the Elites, which means they know our location. So believe me, when I say we need to evacuate, I don't say this lightly."

I couldn't believe how honest and direct Finn was being about everything. Historic figures I'd read about—at least those in politics—were often known for being deceitful and untrustworthy.

The man's wife approached him, placing a gentle hand on his large veiny arm. I wasn't certain if she was trying to tell him to back off, or if she intended to support her husband in standing up to Finn and the others. He reached for her hand and smiled down at her as if to say, *Don't worry, sweetheart, everything will be fine.*

Everything would not be fine. The Elites knew where we were, and the Woodfaces were after us, too. Maybe evacuation wasn't such a bad idea. Or, maybe it was time to let me go. The thought made me sick to my stomach, but as I watched young children hide behind their mothers with big eyes and trembling lips, I couldn't help but feel responsible. If I'd never come here, maybe none of this would have happened.

The man kissed his wife's forehead and moved away from her. Without warning, he clenched a fist and pumped it into the air. "This is our land! We will stay and fight!"

"Fight! Fight! Fight!" others started.

Reina's Champions joined in on the chanting, punching the air with every shout. But the second she shot them a glance, they went silent. It was impressive how much people respected Reina.

The man with long, scraggly hair looked behind him as if upset that everyone had given up taking a stand. "Why are we running? We have men and women capable of fighting. We have trained soldiers. Isn't that why you train our Champions? To protect us? Give me a sword and I'll fight!"

His wife reached for him, but he pulled away.

"We aren't ready to fight," Finn said. "If the Elites get involved, there's no telling what kind of weaponry they might use."

People were already panicking, so I decided it was best to keep my mouth shut about the obliteration guns. If, at some point, Finn needed more help persuading them, I'd deliver the information.

"Then why are they after us all of a sudden?" the man asked. "We've been here for decades, and for the most part, we've lived in peace. What's changed? What are they after?"

Now, I understood why he spoke on behalf of the people. The man was smart, and he knew which questions to ask.

Before Finn could even answer, a few eyes shifted my way.

Finn glanced sideways at Maz, then over at Reina. They must have discussed this very topic inside Finn's house. But what had they decided? I froze, my feet like pillars in the dirt.

When Finn didn't respond, Reina cleared her throat and took a few steps forward with her horse. Her eyes locked on me, and I knew it was over. "They want the girl."

CHAPTER 20

T he girl?"

"What girl?"

"*The* girl."

Slowly, more eyes rolled my way. Some bulged, others narrowed.

"The girl who refused immortality," came a breathy voice.

"Why would they want her?" someone else cried.

"We don't have all the answers," Finn said. "We know for certain that the Woodfaces want Silver—they made a written statement. As for the Elites, we can't be sure. We are only speculating at this time."

"You think that floating white thing was looking for the girl?" someone asked.

"The Eye," Finn corrected. "It has monitored the fields outside of Ortus for years, but recently, it flew over Death Valley. And now, it has entered our home. It has seen us, and knows where we are."

"So it's *her* fault?" came that same breathy voice. An old woman stepped out from the crowd, her large round knees trembling with every step. She pointed a crooked, shaking finger at me. "Then give 'er to them!"

Without warning, Sadie stepped in front of me, puffing out her chest. "Over my dead body."

I parted my lips to say something, even though I wasn't sure what, when Dax also sidestepped to shield me from the crowd. "And mine."

Next, Danika came rushing through the crowd, shoving people out of her way. "And mine!" She panted as she hurried beside Dax.

Rose's dark face emerged from the crowd. Scowling at everyone, she walked briskly over to our group and planted her feet next to mine. She didn't have to say anything for the crowd to know she was serious about taking a stand.

A few people seemed taken aback by this, but then something unexpected happened.

One by one, more Champions formed a barricade around me. Small gusts of wind swept through my hair as people pumped their fists in the air. "The girl who refused! The girl who refused!"

More and more people began chanting those words, their voices spreading through

Ortus like thunder.

"The girl who refused!"

"The girl who refused!"

"The girl who refused!"

Finn went to raise his hand again, but Reina stopped him. She watched him with a smirk, almost as if wanting to appreciate the moment in all its glory.

A moment later, Finn raised his hand, and although everyone went quiet, the silence didn't last long. Without warning, someone shrieked at the top of their lungs—a sound that sent shivers through my body. Everyone spun around to locate the screaming woman, and that's when I saw it.

At the back of the crowd and out of Ortus's main entrance came Jayun. He ran toward us with a sword in one hand and dark blood splattered across the bridge of his nose. He breathed in, his chest expanding three times its size, and in an explosive voice, he roared, "We're under attack!"

Women and children began shouting and running in circles.

"Get the children to the back!" Reina yelled. She kicked the sides of her horse and ran toward Jayun. "Everyone else, gear up!"

What was going on? I stared wide-eyed at Jayun, waiting for bombs to descend from the sky, but nothing happened.

"Everyone, inside your homes!" Finn ordered.

He, too, kicked his horse and charged toward Jayun. Just as Reina moved closer to the tunnel entrance, Ortus's second entrance guard came running out. But he only managed to take three steps when an arrow tore through his chest from the back. He froze, with parted lips and a glazed look in his eyes, before taking one last step and falling to his knees.

"No!" someone cried out.

People moved around like bees trying to protect their queen. There was one problem though: no one knew what to do. Children cried and shrieked, some wanting to run and hide in places they shouldn't be, while adults grabbed them and dragged them away from the village.

I froze as Champions ran by me at full speed, their figures rounded as they charged for the fighting grounds.

And that's when it happened.

The first one came out wearing a wooden mask that resembled a demon. It was oval-shaped and elongated, with holes carved out for its eyes at the center. Under the eyes were thick white stripes painted down the rest of the mask, like tears. But the mask didn't look sad—it looked primal, as if it belonged to someone who'd spent their whole life living with wolves. The mask's forehead was twice the size of a regular forehead, and attached at the top were bloodred feathers leaning backward, covering the top of the attacker's head.

Across his back and chest were more wooden plates, large and finely carved with tribal designs. It looked heavy, but it also protected his flesh.

The attacker stepped out into the village, his wood-padded shoulders drawn back and his black, partially concealed eyes scanning the crowd. In his right hand was a longbow constructed of the same wood as his mask—a reddish brown. Around his waist was a grasslike belt that hung in strands over his torn shorts, almost like a skirt. His limbs weren't protected, but with all the padding over his most vulnerable body parts, I wasn't so sure it mattered.

One by one, more versions of this Woodface emerged from the cavern, carrying a multitude of carved weapons such as battle-axes, spears, swords, and large spiked clubs.

The first attacker to have emerged spotted our Champions running toward the field. His head snapped sideways, his beady eyes watching our people run. In one swift motion, he extracted a long arrow from the quiver on his back, loaded his bow, and fired a shot.

The arrow pierced the air and penetrated a young girl's neck, the intense blow propelling her through the air and onto the ground. Several Champions stopped running to try to help her, but it was too late—she was gone.

When the second arrow came hurtling through the air, everyone seemed to understand that stopping wasn't an option. At the same time, another two Woodfaces gripping bows stepped out into the open.

"*Arklas!*" shouted the biggest of them all.

He was the third to emerge, and twice the size of everyone else. In his hand, he held a club spiked with what appeared to be human canine teeth.

I swallowed hard.

He lowered his head, inspecting our village through the tiny holes in his mask, then raised a fist and yelled, "*Firus stiffen!*" and began pointing at different areas in the village.

He stepped off the stone platform outside of the cavern's entrance, his leg muscles looking twice the size of my torso, and continued to give orders. As he spoke, more Woodfaces came pouring out of the cavern, like ants exiting their colony.

How many were there? When would this stop? I searched for Finn and Reina, but they were nowhere to be seen. Had they taken Jayun to safety? How were we supposed to fight such an army?

"Come on!" Sadie shouted.

I looked at her like she was crazy and pointed at the dozen Champions on the ground with arrows protruding from their bodies. "They're firing arrows at anyone trying to get into the grounds! We don't stand a chance!" I said.

She grabbed my shoulders and stared me square in the face. "You're trained to run, remember?"

My heart thudded hard against my rib cage. Trained to run? Was I really expected to run through a death trap?

I stared at the dead bodies, then at the quickly expanding army of Woodfaces. More and more archers came out, preparing their bows.

"We don't have time!" Sadie said.

Without thinking, I charged straight toward the fighting grounds' entrance. The sound of arrows whistled near me as I ran, but I did my best to ignore them. If I focused on the army next to me, I feared I might change my mind and run the opposite way.

I ran fast, feeling like my legs might detach from my body. It felt surreal, like I was floating. Was this really happening? Were we going to war?

"Silver!" Sadie called out in a panic.

I dug my heels into the dirt, and a second later, an arrow came crashing into the ground in front of my toes. One more step and my skull would have been split. I shot Sadie a glance, but she urged me to keep running.

As we entered the fighting grounds, Champions emerged grasping weapons in their hands. Near the stables, Reina rode in circles with her horse, ordering people to gather certain weapons only, and sending certain Champions to the back of the field. I wasn't sure where they were going, but they must have been making their way to an exit I didn't know about. Reina was likely planning to attack from various angles.

People ran as fast as they could, avoiding arrows as they came twirling through the air.

Near the front of the grounds, next to the fence, was a pile of countless weapons. Someone must have gathered them from the back and brought them here.

Sadie ran toward the pile and pulled out two spears.

As I reached for a spear, she froze. But before I could ask her what was wrong, I caught the scent of something.

"Do you smell that?" I asked.

Sadie sniffed the air. "Fire."

"Fire!" someone called out.

"Focus!" Reina shouted.

I gazed over the fence to spot a streak of black smoke floating toward the sky. Stretching my neck, I peeked at the cavern entrance to spot a dozen or so Woodfaces forming a line and lighting their arrowheads on fire. At once, they aimed their fiery tips at the village, waiting.

"*Firus!*" shouted the large Woodface in charge.

Bowstrings snapped, people screamed, and a radiating heat swept through the air as fire arrows rained from the sky.

Without warning, a fireless arrow zipped toward me. Right before it tore through my skull, Sadie grabbed me by the shirt and pulled me back.

"Don't stick your face out in the open like that," she said through clenched teeth.

Around me, Champions suited up—some in leather padded materials, and others in metal meshing.

Sadie grabbed a thin metallic vest from the pile and slipped it over my head. It was a bit too big for me, the shoulder plates sticking out farther than my shoulders, but it would protect me from an arrow to the chest. Sadie went on to suit herself up, loading her belt with knives and sharp objects. Trying to mimic her, I reached for a weapons belt on the ground. But as I bent forward, she grabbed me by my new vest and pulled me upright.

"No," she stated and pointed at the stables. "Go in there and hide."

"What?" I exclaimed. "Why? I can fight. Let me fight."

"No!" she lashed out. "Don't you get it? They're here for you, Silver."

I stared at her, eyes wide. "How—"

Champions brushed past me, some shouting and others pointing toward the Woodfaces as they ran into battle. Cries echoed all around us, but all I could focus on was Sadie and the spears piled up next to me.

"We didn't give in to their demands, and now they're coming for you," she said.

I reached for a spear again and she grabbed me firmly by the arms. Her grasp was solid and unforgiving. "No!" she hissed. "If they get you, this will all have been for nothing. You're a beacon of hope, Silver. We need you alive."

It all sounded ridiculous to me. Why were they fighting so hard to keep me? People were dying—because of me! Clenching my teeth, I stared at her, refusing to back down.

"I want to fight," I said.

She shook me hard. "I don't have time for this. Get in that stable—that's an order."

I wasn't sure if my anger toward the Elites and the Woodfaces is what propelled me to fight, or if it was my wanting to remain by

Sadie's side. I didn't want her running into battle. What if something happened?

She pointed at the stables menacingly and I did as instructed. The longer I stood there arguing with her, the more lives I risked. Arrows whistled nearby as I charged across the field, dodging Champions and a large, broad-shouldered Woodface as he entered the fighting grounds.

They were gaining on us.

He walked into the field, swinging a large wooden sword over his head and increasing momentum. With a deep, rumbly roar, he spun in a circle one more time before batting his sword at one of our Champions. The young man cried out, his voice piercing my ears as I ran by, and the sound of crunching echoed around me—shattering ribs.

The young Champion collapsed, and the Woodface went on to roaring and swinging his massive weapon at others.

But I didn't look back.

I ran as fast as I could, my heart pounding so hard I thought my chest might explode. I focused my gaze on the empty stable's muddy floor and bales of hay, trying to ignore the cries of agony and the dark blood splattering behind me.

But everything was so loud.

People screamed—some in terror, others in

pain or rage. In the distance came shrill cries that told me innocent lives were being taken. I peered through a crack in the stable to spot Finn swaying wildly back and forth on his horse as he rode, swinging what appeared to be a long metal sword stained in red.

Every few seconds, Reina ran across the scene, her mouth a gaping hole and she released war cries.

Where was Sadie?

Suddenly, a spear tore through a Woodface's chest.

Sadie.

Why weren't they slowing down? More Woodfaces emerged from the cavern, pumped up and ready to fight. How many of them were there?

"No!" Reina shouted.

I inched closer to the stable wall, pressing my face against the wood to get a good look.

Reina was yelling at someone, but I couldn't tell who. She pointed at the person, then kicked the sides of her horse and charged toward them. I shifted my angle and caught a glimpse of Finn moving fast toward the cavern entrance.

He sat with his shoulders slouched forward as if trying to pierce through the thick air. What was he going to do? Trample our enemies? It wouldn't work. There were too many of them. But as he drew in near—and as a dozen Woodfaces aimed their sharp weapons at him—he did something I never imagined possible.

He propped himself up onto the back of his horse, his feet planted firmly on its saddle. And right as the Woodfaces attempted to jab him with their weapons, he jumped as high as he could—over their heads, and toward the cavern entrance.

As he came back down toward the stone ground, he tossed something inside the dark tunnel. Countless Woodfaces turned to look inside, seemingly shocked by whatever it was Finn had thrown. He landed somewhere in the crowd of our enemies, but I didn't hear a sound. Everyone was shouting, grunting, or crying.

A female Woodface lowered her head to look at him through her mask's slits, and prepared a spear over her head for a final blow.

But before she could strike, a deafening sound erupted from behind her. It sounded like thunder—like the cracking of lightning in the worst storm imaginable. At the same time, a huge ball of smoke, fire, and debris came blasting out of the tunnel, sending countless Woodfaces flying in every direction.

Then, the earth shook, as did the mountains. Everything trembled so intensely that I felt it in the stable's wooden structure. Another loud rumbling sound erupted, and this time, the tunnel collapsed on itself, crushing whoever remained inside.

CHAPTER 21

Pieces of rock rolled and bounced down the mountain, and a fine white powder burst into the air.

Some of those who had been thrown away by the explosion slowly sat up, holding on to their heads while trying to make sense of what had happened. Others didn't move at all. Our Champions immediately took advantage of the situation, slaying Woodfaces on the ground before they could even stand.

It may not have been fair, but neither was invading our home.

One nearby Woodface sat up without a mask, and that was when I saw it—his scars.

His face, a bubbly red, made it look as though someone had dunked him inside a pot of boiling water as a child. It was terrifying to look at, like something out of a horror story. In a daze, he reached for his mask and slid it back on. Right when it went back into place, a young man came charging at him with a club and smashed him on the side of the head. The mask flew off again, and red feathers detached and blew into the wind. Blood splattered toward the floating feathers and the Woodface collapsed to his side.

"Finn!" Reina cried out.

She ran toward the pile of debris, climbed off her horse, and began lifting large rocks. Others joined, helping her clear the pile.

The war cries spreading throughout Ortus began to subside. In its place came lamenting and sobbing. Fire crackled in the distance as wooden houses collapsed.

And what was I doing? Hiding behind a pile of hay? Watching the terror unfold from safety?

This was wrong. I needed to help somehow.

I rushed out of the stable, nearly tripping over a dead body in the field. The woman was young—maybe early twenties—and lay still with a blank stare fixated on the fast-approaching clouds.

"Sadie!" I called out.

People ran back and forth, some dragging injured bodies, others landing final blows on our enemies to ensure they were dead. Over the fence, black smoke rose into the sky, joining the dark gray clouds.

"Sadie!" I tried again.

"Everyone to the village!" someone nearby shouted. I'd seen him before—maybe a second- or third-in-command—but I'd never spoken to him. He was tall, slender, and had a large, crooked nose that seemed the result of a recent break. He spoke as if Reina herself had put him in charge.

Maybe she had.

"Bring citizens to safety!" he ordered. "Gather as many buckets of water as you can and fight the flames. If you see any Woodfaces alive, I want them dead."

I gazed up at the sky. If we were lucky, it would rain soon.

Everyone ran past me as if I were invisible. They sprinted out of the field, turning the corner to assist survivors within the village.

As the crowd scattered, I moved toward the explosion's aftermath. Maybe Sadie had gone to help find Finn.

"Sadie!" I tried again.

Where was she? Had something happened? My stomach sank. What if she'd been killed? What if I stumbled on her lifeless body? I searched the grass, hoping I wouldn't find her pale face. I couldn't believe how many dead bodies lay everywhere. The fight had been a complete massacre.

We'd been caught off guard, unprepared.

It was only thanks to Finn that the

Woodfaces hadn't managed to take out the entire village.

I stepped over a female Woodface with a missing arm—a bloody stump—and opened my mouth to call Sadie's name out again. But before I could say anything, a deep grunt resonated from behind me.

I swung around in time to find a large, tan man staring at me from behind his mask. With legs at shoulder's width, he stood still with a rounded back and bent, bloody fingers like an animal about to pounce. He'd lost his armor but seemed unconcerned. His chest and abdomen were so chiseled it made me wonder whether an arrow would even pierce his skin. He held no weapon, but it was clear to me that he didn't need one for what he intended to do.

With those veiny, rust-colored hands, he'd tear me to shreds. I took a step back, pondering whether running was the best course of action. I had no weapon, either, and the Champions at the field's entrance only seconds ago had all run off to help civilians.

Where had this Woodface even come from? The fighting grounds were empty.

Although I couldn't see the killer behind the mask, I got the feeling he was smiling at me. It was as if he felt that having found me meant the war wasn't over. He took a step forward, when one of his red feathers detached from his bloodstained mask and floated down into the grass.

I glanced at the pile of weapons near the gate—specifically at a spear lying on its side—and his eyes followed mine.

I could try, but something told me he'd catch me before I even had the chance to pick something up. The man was large, but not overly thick. He was lean, and well-defined, which told me that on top of possessing great strength, he was likely fast, too.

With a deep breath, I took another step back, and he tilted his head at me. It was a look that translated to *Go ahead and try*.

Without thinking, I did exactly that.

I ran as fast and as hard as I could, charging toward Reina. If there was one person I knew could fire a lethal blow from a distance, it was her.

"Reina!" I called out.

At the sound of my voice, she didn't turn her head or flinch. She was too busy trying to locate Finn from underneath all the debris. She climbed up on a large bolder, pointed below, and shouted orders to five young men and women who went on to lift a huge rock out of the way.

From behind, rapid footsteps charged for me, stomping on the ground as they came closer.

He was too fast. Although I ran with everything I had, it sounded like with each step I took, the Woodface took three. Something shiny caught my eye.

A sword.

It lay still in the grass with dead fingers wrapped around its leather handle. Its blade, covered in dark blood, looked black as it reflected the dangerous overhead clouds.

If I acted quickly enough, I might stand a chance.

The footsteps drew nearer and my heart nearly climbed into my throat. Adrenaline burst through me, and although everything was happening so fast, it almost felt like time was slowing. Right when I felt he was behind me, I slid through the grass, landing next to the dead body.

I shook uncontrollably as I fought to pry the fingers away from the sword. It wasn't a difficult task, but I was so unnerved that I couldn't think clearly. I couldn't think much at all. The only thing I could do was act.

Suddenly, a forceful grunt filled the air behind me—something I could have easily mistaken for thunder. I rolled onto my back with the sword held firmly in both fists, its sharp blade aimed at my attacker as he lunged at me.

Everything happened so quickly that I

didn't realize what was going on until pain and immense pressure jabbed me in the stomach. At first, the pain was slow and gradual, but it quickly became intolerable.

I breathed hard, my chest barely heaving. What happened? Had I dropped the sword?

No, I still held on to it. I tried to move my hands, but they were stuck under the weight of the Woodface's dead body. He lay on top of me, motionless, as warm blood trickled from his stomach and onto my hands around the sword's handle.

The handle.

That was where the pain was coming from. He was so heavy that he'd forced my handle into my stomach. I tried to shift sideways, hoping he might topple over, but I couldn't move. I couldn't breathe.

"Help—" It came out quiet and breathy.

"Silver!"

Someone yanked the body off me, and at my feet stood Dax, covered in blood from head to toe. She breathed hard, her muscular shoulders bouncing up and down, and extended me a hand. I immediately dropped the sword and reached for her.

The second she pulled me up, I winced and reached for my stomach.

"You okay?" she asked. "Let me see."

I raised my shirt to reveal a shallow

puncture wound from the sword's handle. Around it, my skin was already bruising and red from broken blood vessels. I breathed out, thankful for the chainmail vest Sadie had thrown over my head.

"Is that from—" She aimed her gaze at the sword.

I kept my hand pressed on the painful area and nodded.

Slowly, a grin stretched the lower half of her square face. What was she smiling about? She ran a hand through her short, muddy hair, then wiped a streak of blood off her chin.

"Gotta say, Silver, that was pretty badass. Didn't think you had it in you."

I wasn't sure what she was implying. Was it because I was smaller framed than she was? I was training to be a Champion, same as her. I must have scowled. She patted my shoulder and added, "It's not an insult, Silver. Not everyone is cut out for battle. Everyone knows you're a symbol of hope, but no one's ever seen you fight."

Only then did I realize that many people had stopped what they were doing. They stared my way, silent. I glanced down at my shirt, which was soaked in our enemy's blood. My hands trembled, so I placed them at my sides, hoping it wouldn't show.

"That monster you just killed took five

innocent lives at the back of the village," Dax said. "He went on a rampage. Three women and two boys."

I ground my teeth, wanting to pick up the sword and stab him again.

"He must have snuck around the village's perimeter," Dax continued. "No one could find him. But you got him."

I wanted to say that it was circumstantial. It wasn't as if I'd hunted him down like some trained warrior. The Woodface had attacked *me*. I'd simply defended myself, and the only reason I won was because of dumb luck.

"We got him!" someone called out.

Dozens of people gathered around the pile of broken rocks and debris near what had once been Ortus's entrance. Now, it was nothing more than a slanted wall of stone. How would we fix this? Was there anything left to fix, or was it all gone? Had we lost our primary entrance?

"Pull!" Reina shouted, yanking hard on what looked to be someone's arm.

Around her, soldiers dug spears and swords underneath a large, uneven rock, pushing the weight of their bodies downward as if trying to activate a lever. It seemed to work. With every new person joining in on the mission, the rock shifted higher, and higher, until finally, Reina managed to drag a torn and bloody version of

Finn out from underneath.

He didn't move or speak, and as people rushed around him, Reina urged them to back away. "Give him space!" She then clicked her fingers and two medics wearing navy blue attire with red patches on their sleeves came running toward her, carrying a makeshift bamboo stretcher. They carefully lowered it onto a flat surface and knelt by Finn, assessing his wounds.

I'd never seen Reina so frightened before. She watched the medics as if watching them perform open-heart surgery. When the medics nodded and mumbled something, Reina blew out a long breath.

Finn was alive.

"Silver!" came Sadie's voice.

I spun around. She ran toward Dax and me with her messy, blood-soaked hair tied in an unkempt bun at the back of her head. Her lips pulled sideways every few seconds as if she was combating a smile. Either that, or tears.

"You're okay," she breathed.

I wanted to say the same, but she stepped close to me and held me by the shoulders, examining my face. "Are you okay?" She searched every inch of me as if the thought of a single bruise would be enough to infuriate her.

I didn't bring up the bruise on my belly or

the Woodface who had nearly killed me.

"I'm okay. What about you?"

She didn't respond, and instead, stared into me for what felt like minutes. Her blue eyes looked like little planets full of stars around them. I smiled, losing myself in her beauty.

"I thought I lost you," she said. "Someone mentioned you were attacked—"

I pointed at the bloody sword in the grass. "No, I'm okay. I defended myself."

Her brows met above her nose. "What were you even doing out here? I told you to stay in the stables."

"I couldn't see you anywhere," I said. "I got worried and wanted to come help."

She breathed out hard through flared nostrils. "You could have gotten yourself—"

"Killed," I cut her off. "I know. But I couldn't sit around doing nothing—"

"Right now, you can," she said coldly. "Since you've been here, we've gathered an additional thirty recruits. People look up to you, Silver. If you're dead, things might not keep progressing the way they've been."

I kept my mouth shut. I understood the politics behind it, but it didn't sit right with me. How could I hide while others fought to the death to protect me? It was so wrong. But arguing with Sadie wouldn't get me anywhere.

"I understand," I said simply.

Sighing, she rubbed my shoulder. "You sure you're okay?"

For a moment, I stared at her bright eyes, her pronounced cheekbones, her plush pink lips... What was wrong with me? Why couldn't I stop staring? Better yet, why couldn't she stop, either?

I wanted to reach for her face, caress her, something.

She made her eyes go so big that I spun around, expecting to find an enemy charging our way. There was no one.

"Sadie, what—" I started, but when she reached for her bloody belly, I saw it.

Out from under her rib cage was the tip of an arrowhead. Around it, her clothes began to soak up so much blood that it looked like paint spilling across a flat surface.

"No, no, no," I said, feeling like my words weren't my own.

Everything around me spun, and Sadie collapsed to her knees.

"No, please, Sadie." I grabbed her shoulders, shaking her. I didn't know what to do. Her terrified eyes softened into their natural almond shape, and she watched me quietly as I panicked. How was she so calm?

"It's okay," she breathed.

It wasn't okay. It was far from okay. I wasn't about to lose my best friend.

"No, it's not!" I cried. "You can't die!" I shook her again, but stopped when Dax grabbed my shoulder firmly. I wasn't helping. If anything, I was probably hurting her.

She smiled sweetly at me and reached for my cheek. It was the sweetest touch I'd ever felt and I didn't want it to end. My throat swelled and warm tears drizzled down my face. I wasn't ready. I couldn't lose her.

She parted her lips to say something, but nothing came out. Her eyelids fluttered, and her fingers grazed my cheek as she slipped away and fell to the ground.

Around me, the fiery village spun several times. In the distance came cries of mourning as people ran throughout all of Ortus, searching for loved ones. But it all sounded so distorted, as if I were underwater.

This wasn't real.

I was dreaming.

Any second now, Sadie would wake me up and tell me it was time to start my training.

Any second now…

As my eyes rolled up from Sadie's motionless body, I spotted a figure near the fighting grounds. He walked in rapid circles, searching the grass with his mask aimed at the ground. The tilt caused the mask's feathers to topple forward.

He searched with rounded shoulders and a

snapping head, like a wild animal. In his right hand was a bow, but his other hand was empty.

What was he looking for? Arrows?

And then it hit me.

He'd been the one to kill Sadie. He was responsible.

Dax said something, but I was too out of it to hear her. All I could think about was this Woodface, and how I wanted to rip out his throat. Bending down, I grabbed Sadie's spear. I took a few steps to gain my strength, and with a roar, hurled it straight at the Woodface.

He must have heard my voice and glanced up in time to see who had taken the shot, but he didn't have enough time to dodge my attack. The spear spun fast toward his face, shattering his mask instantly. It tore through his right eye—a wet squishing sound that was barely audible over the shattering of bone—and split through his skull. The blow had been so hard that I was surprised it didn't take his head clean off.

Propelled backward, he landed hard on his back. As I stared at his lifeless body and at the spear sticking straight up, I didn't feel guilty. I should have. I'd taken a second life, now. But this man was a monster, and he deserved every bit of pain he felt. If anything, I wanted to walk up to him and rip out the spear to inflict more pain, if he was even still alive.

240

What was wrong with me?

Why did I feel so much anger and hatred?

I glanced down at Sadie, my heart feeling like it might give out. I wanted to crumble next to her and sob, but Dax gave me a look that told me I didn't have time to grieve. Later, I could break down for having lost a friend.

As smoke swept through the village, filling our lungs, people ran toward the river with cloths over their faces. Some tried to stop the flames, but it was no use. They'd taken over. I watched in horror as houses collapsed, the cracking and snapping sounds bouncing off the mountains around us.

People sobbed as bodies were carried away from the thickening smoke. Medics couldn't keep up. Some people screamed, begging for help with an injured loved one, but there weren't enough medics.

We only had a few.

No one had expected a massacre of this magnitude.

I stared at the scenery before me, frozen.

Dax ran off toward Finn and Reina and pointed my way. What was she telling them? That I was broken? That I couldn't move? How long had I been standing there, anyway?

"You!" someone shouted at me. "Help us with carrying supplies!"

My eyes slowly rolled upward, where

countless people of all ages ran in and out of our barn, carrying with them bags of wheat, beans, flour, and more. One fire arrow had penetrated the roof, and flames slowly licked at a corner window, but we still had time. Minutes, maybe, before the roof risked collapsing.

I blinked hard, glanced down at Sadie's body one last time, and ran toward the barn.

CHAPTER 22

Everyone looked scared.

Mothers held on to their children, pulling them tight against their chests as Reina trotted back and forth with her horse. She shouted commands, pointing at anyone she could.

Everything was chaos.

We weren't prepared for this. When Finn mentioned a migration, I didn't imagine this. I pictured something a bit slower—something more well-planned. But as people lined up at the back of the village, along the tall wooden fence, I couldn't help but wonder how many of us would even survive. We'd only managed to extract half of our food supply from the barn, and everyone looked emotionally defeated.

Two arms grabbed me around the shoulders and I stiffened, prepared to strike a blow.

"You okay?" someone asked.

I spotted Danika's red hair in my peripheral. She hugged me, but I was too dazed to hug her back.

"I heard what happened," she said.

I parted my lips, but nothing came out.

Her watering sea-green eyes stared into me before rolling down toward my abdomen. "You're hurt."

I reached for my stomach. It was warm and wet. I'd been so preoccupied thinking about what happened to Sadie that I'd forgotten all about my injury. When I pulled my fingers up to eye level, they were red and silky.

"What happened?" Danika asked.

I couldn't remember. At least, not the details.

"Attack," I said simply.

What was this? Shock? I couldn't think clearly. Everything felt like an illusion.

I blinked hard, trying to regain focus. Danika patted my shoulder. "You should have that checked out as soon as possible."

Although I nodded, I had no intention of getting medical help. Ortus's medics were busy enough trying to save lives. I'd overheard someone say that while we were migrating, the critically injured would have to stay here until they were stable enough to migrate to wherever it was we were going.

"If there's anything you need—" Danika

said.

"It's her fault," someone growled.

I turned sideways toward a middle-aged woman who glowered at me with such ferocity I wondered if maybe she was a Woodface without her mask. But she wore normal hemp clothing like the rest of us.

Who was she pointing at? Me?

"Back off," Danika said.

An older man stepped forward as if trying to protect the woman. Maybe it was her husband.

"Forty-two souls lost today," the man growled. "Forty-two! Why? Because of her!" He jabbed his finger my way and curled his lips over his teeth.

"Her fault?" Danika said. "A few hours ago, you were all chanting her name!"

"That was before she got a bunch of us killed!" came another voice.

Slowly, the lineup broke apart and began forming a semicircle around me. Some people simply scowled, while others shouted insults and shook their fists at me.

"Back off!" Danika shouted again.

"You killed my brother!" came another voice.

This one had sounded much closer. I tried to spin around to see who'd shouted at me, but something hard suddenly crashed into me, throwing me into the grass. On top of me was a girl around my age. She had unkempt blond hair tied to one side and bared her teeth at me like a vicious animal.

At once, she raised a solid fist.

She came down at me hard, knocking me in the cheek, the forehead, and the chin. My brain shook with every swing, and by the time I raised my arms to protect myself, she'd already hit me enough times for everything to go blurry.

"Hey!" came a deep, thunderous voice.

Someone immediately dragged the girl off me and threw her into the crowd.

"You okay?"

Dax hovered over me, a blue vein bulging in the middle of her red forehead.

"If any of you try that again," she shouted, her blurred figure moving toward the crowd, "so help me God—"

"Enough!" Reina shouted. "What's going on here?"

The sound of hooves against earth echoed nearby.

"We've had enough losses today," Reina growled. "You should be ashamed of yourselves for turning on one of your own!"

Although only one person had physically attacked me, I got the feeling she was directing her anger at everyone around in the crowd.

From the ground, she looked huge on her horse. Distorted, even. I blinked hard and rubbed the side of my head, confused.

"She isn't one of our own!" someone said.

Reina went quiet for a moment, and I imagined her biting her lip, holding back a slew of insults.

"I understand today has been extremely difficult for all of us," she said calmly. "But blaming the girl isn't the answer. She may be wanted by the Elites, but she didn't ask for this to happen. Silverstasia Blackwood is the first person to ever stand up to the injustices imposed by the Elites. It's no wonder they want her. They'll do anything to put a stop to those wanting to rebel against their ways. While you may have lived a comfortable life here in Ortus, unaware of the monstrosities happening in Lutum, it doesn't make the injustices any less real. People are being used as slaves over there. Don't you see that? Doesn't that bother you? We're better than this. What if those were your children in Lutum?" She paused and pointed at a few people. "What if your daughter was selected to become a breeder? To be basically raped and forced to bear children for the Elites? Would you be okay with that? Are you so selfish that you're willing to ignore what's been happening because you don't *personally* know the people of Lutum? Because they aren't blood relatives?"

Everyone remained quiet. With how furious Reina sounded, I wasn't so sure how she'd react if someone dared speak out now. I sat up, my vision slowly regaining its focus. A few people looked away from me, and others bowed their heads shamefully.

"This is the price of war," Reina growled. "The Elites will never stop, and while you might think you're safe outside of their territory—think again. They could decide to enslave all of us at any point. They were bold enough to send another clan onto our territory—all for one girl. They're desperate. They're afraid, and they should be. Because of Silver, people are rising. Imagine what they'll do if their own people rebel against them. If they run out of slaves? They already massacred an entire division. They'll come hunting for more."

Reina's horse kicked the ground as if it agreed with her words.

"If you want to point fingers and blame others, point them at yourselves. Finn has been warning all of you for decades that war with the Elites was inevitable. While we're thankful to all the young men and women who signed up to become Champions, many of you didn't." She glared at the crowd, specifically at the younger able-bodied people. "And it wasn't until Silver showed up that we had an influx in enlistments. If her being here hadn't motivated so many people to become Champions, none of us would have survived today's attack. And if we hadn't been attacked today, we would have, eventually. It was only a matter of time."

A cool breeze swept past us, whistling as it ran along the fence.

Dax offered me a hand, so I grabbed it, and she yanked me back up onto my feet. I felt queasy and unstable, but she held me firmly in place.

"You okay?" she whispered.

I nodded, and it hurt my head.

"I now ask that anyone who is physically capable of lifting objects, please help us load everything into the carts. Maz is setting everything up, and the horses will be here shortly. We'll be opening the back gates once we're ready to start the migration."

An elderly woman raised her hand, her fingertips twitching as if too weak against even the slightest breeze. "Wh-where are we going, if you don't mind my asking?"

Reina sat up straight on her horse, her back rigid and shoulders drawn back. "We have a refugee camp about thirty miles from here. There, we'll find allies, some beds, and a place to camp out for the next few days. This will give us time to treat our wounded and determine the next best course of action."

No one spoke, but I got the feeling we were all thinking the same thing—what would happen next? Were we expected to build another city? Would we scavenge the land in search of a preexisting village? There was so much uncertainty. No wonder everyone was on edge.

Lyla and Lyson emerged from the crowd, their almost-translucent blond hair looking brown beneath the black sky. Any minute now, the clouds would tear open, soaking all of us from head to toe.

"I can help," Lyson said.

When he caught me staring, he smiled at me—a look that said, *I'm glad to see you're alive.*

I tried to smile back, but I couldn't. His sister, Lyla, nudged her brother out of the way and started walking toward the oncoming carts. I hadn't noticed them until then. Along the tall fence of the fighting grounds came four horse-drawn carts, each of them the size of a house.

The first cart was driven by Maz, who stared ahead with a scowl—a look of concentration that told me she meant business. Behind her, the other three followed close, the horses neighing and nickering as they pulled.

"Civilians in the first two carts," Reina ordered as Maz approached.

Maz nodded and spat something out of her mouth, then got up from the driver's seat and dropped down into the grass. "All right, folks," she said. "Start loading the last two carts with essential supplies only. Toys, furniture, and everything else will have to wait until our second trip."

"Second trip?" someone mumbled.

Lyla was the first to grab a tin can of wheat. While many of our supplies seemed to be in bags, a lot more sat in containers—I imagined this was for long-term storage. Her brother quickly ran behind her, following suit. And one by one, others joined in, bringing supplies into the carts at the back. Women, children, and the elderly were guided to climb into the first carts, while the younger generation and middle-aged men took part in the heavy lifting.

"Not that, sweetheart," one woman told her little girl. She tugged on the girl's stuffed animal—a purple giraffe with a sagging neck—trying to pry it from her little hands, but the girl pulled away and cried as if holding on to her best friend. The mother looked at Maz desperately, who simply shook her head as if to say, "It's fine. Let her keep it."

Lightning flashed overhead, and crackling thunder followed. The little girl retreated into the pit of her mother's arm. Finally, the clouds burst open, and down came heavy rainfall.

Some people cowered from it, while others stood with gaping mouths, allowing the rain to clean blood and dirt off their skin.

One by one, more people climbed into the cart, many of them looking weak, tired, and filthy from soot and dirt. One older gentleman slipped on the wet surface, nearly falling backward before two young Champions helped him up. It was painful to watch. These helpless people were leaving behind what they knew as their home, with no idea as to where they were going to live next.

Would they adapt? It wasn't like we had a choice.

As Lyla and Lyson came back, I took a step toward them, prepared to start grabbing supplies. But before I could go anywhere, Reina called out to me.

"Not you. You're needed elsewhere."

Needed elsewhere? Where could I possibly be needed?

"Hop on," she ordered.

I did as she'd told me and climbed onto the back of her horse. Without a word, she led us back into the village. The heavy rain had killed off the fire, leaving behind what looked like the aftermath of a bomb. Everything looked dark and dreary, but there was no smoke, nor bright orange flames dancing out the open windows.

Everything looked dead.

I stared at the hospital cabin as we walked past it, noting how intact it was. It was about five times the size of a regular home, with two stories and several small windows forming rows across its wooden frame. It reminded me of images I'd seen of old Catholic churches, only there were no crosses or stained glass. The building was constructed of the same wood as everything else in the village. What surprised me most of all was how clean and unbeaten it looked. The only damage to it was the corner of its roof, which had burned off. Meanwhile, the houses next to it had burned to a crisp.

"How did that happen?" I asked, pointing at the hospital.

"Priority," Reina said, gently guiding her horse over a burnt beam. "We may not be as advanced as the Elites, but we do have quite a bit of medical equipment. Everyone was ordered to keep the fire away from the hospital."

I stared at the empty wooden buckets of water lying around the hospital's perimeter, wondering how many people had participated in fighting the flames. I hadn't helped at all. I'd been too busy standing over Sadie's still body.

Swallowing hard, I pushed the thought away. If I allowed it to consume me, I might break down.

Reina brought us to the least damaged house in all of Ortus. Although black burn marks ran along its exterior walls, the structure itself seemed fine.

What were we doing here? My heart pounded as Reina climbed down and told me to follow. Were they planning on leaving me behind? Sacrificing me for what had happened? Why was I even having these ridiculous thoughts?

I followed her into the darkness of the small house, feeling vulnerable. But at the same time, I knew that if there was one person I could trust more than Sadie, it was Reina. She was, after all, a mother figure to Sadie.

Did she not know what had happened? Why wasn't she shedding a tear? I wanted to ask her if she was aware of the loss, but it wasn't the right time. Maybe, like me, she was holding everything in.

The moment we entered the house, I spotted two figures—one lying awkwardly on the bed against the back wall, and another sitting on a chair in the kitchen area.

I blinked hard, my eyes adjusting to the dim lighting.

"Silver," came Finn's voice.

I blinked again. Finn? How could it be?

"Finn?" I asked.

The figure on the bed sat up slowly, and

Finn's face came into view. It was battered and swollen, and his left eye was puffy and sealed shut. Around his neck was a white cotton material that hung down in front of his chest, holding his arm in place. He winced and grumbled as he straightened his position.

"You're alive," I said, matter-of-factly.

He laughed but then groaned. "Y-yeah. Thanks to Reina here."

"Don't sound too happy about it," Reina said.

Finn tried to smile—a noticeable twitch of the lips. I couldn't even imagine the amount of pain he was in. He'd been crushed under rock and debris. I'd seen it for myself. How was he still breathing?

The other figure coughed, and when I turned to look at who sat next to me, I nearly jumped back into Reina. I could tell it was a Woodface by the way it was dressed—a grasslike draping around its body, rope around its waist, wooden armor on its shoulders and across its chest, and tall suede boots that looked to be over a decade old.

But what gave it away was his face. Like the other Woodface I'd seen, this man had scars on his face. It was a shame. Only half looked red and disfigured, while the other half was decent-looking with a fascinating golden eye and olive skin. The burn scars were so bad that they had melted his hair follicles on the right side, making him look hideous. He breathed hard through his deformed lips—a sound that only amplified his monstrous appearance—and stared at me with wide, hungry eyes.

Why was he looking at me like that?

He grunted, kicked the floor, and shook his body violently, causing the chair to wobble from side to side. But he was tied up with his hands behind his back. His ankles, too, were shackled to the chair.

Why was he even here?

"We kept one alive," Finn said, his voice low and rumbly.

I wondered if he'd punctured a lung or broken some ribs.

"What for?" I asked.

Finn shifted the weight of his body to his other side. "For answers."

"We want to know why they attacked," Reina said.

"I thought—" I started, prepared to blame myself for the attack.

"We had our assumptions," Finn said. "But I wanted a definitive answer."

"Did you get it?" I asked, my heart pounding hard.

Although I already felt responsible for this, I was terrified to receive confirmation. If this Woodface confirmed that they'd massacred so many people because of me, I wasn't sure how I would cope with that.

"He refuses to cooperate," Finn said. With difficulty, he stood up and grabbed onto what appeared to be a wooden staff.

Reina hurried to his side, but he gestured her away.

Seeing Finn this way made me sick to my stomach. Only hours ago, he'd been such a strong and capable leader. Now, he could barely stand on his own.

"Come," he said, walking past Reina and me.

I wrinkled my brow. "But I thought—"

Reina shook her head as a way of saying, *Don't question Finn.*

We stepped out into the rain, which had turned into a fine drizzle. Finn pressed his cheek against his staff and stared off into the village. He stood there for several minutes, taking in the devastating scene.

I couldn't tell if he wanted to cry, scream, or collapse to his knees. It gutted me.

I remembered seeing the pictures in Finn's stairway—the ones depicting images from decades ago, when they'd first begun to build the village of Ortus. Now, everything Finn and his people had worked so hard for was destroyed.

"You're special, Silver," Finn said without looking at me.

Special? I felt the opposite of special as I stood there amid crumbled houses, burned wood, shattered glass, and melted furniture I could no longer recognize.

He turned to look at me. "He recognized you."

I must have crinkled my nose. Finn smirked, regripped his staff, and added, "The Woodface. He recognized you."

Reina and I stood silently. Still, I didn't understand what he was telling me, so I waited.

"That's the only confirmation I needed," he said.

Slowly, he turned away from us and started limping toward the hospital, his bare feet squishing through the mud.

I locked eyes with Reina. It all made sense now. The Eye, the Woodfaces, they were connected. The only way a Woodface would have known anything about me, or what I looked like, was if the Elites had given them my information, and my location, which they'd obtained using the Eye.

The Elites had done this, and they would pay dearly.

CHAPTER 23

When we walked into the hospital, it smelled of ash, blood, sweat, and dirt. A hint of lemon lingered nearby, but the rusty smell of blood overpowered it.

I stood silently as Reina spoke with doctors dressed in long white coats. A few other people wore outfits made of blue fabric, and it was only when Reina referred to them as nurses that I knew what their roles were.

Their clothes looked faded like they'd worn the same ones for years. Maybe they'd looted them from an abandoned hospital, along with all the other equipment in here.

Cries and moans filled the space, mostly coming from behind closed curtains. The layout was cramped and chaotic, but I imagined it wasn't always that way. It looked like they'd pulled beds out of storage to accommodate the unexpected influx of patients in need of critical care.

Patients lay side by side, their bandages soaked in blood. Some were conscious, others, sound asleep. Nurses scrambled in every direction. A few were shouting over the motionless bodies, while others pointed at the medics and demanded medication.

It was a mess.

One of the doctors—a tall woman with silvery blond hair and a rounded back—guided Finn away from the crowd and toward the back of the large building. Had they saved him a bed? Probably.

Reina turned around and joined me at the entrance.

Seeing all the blood, the torment, and the broken bones made me queasy... and guilty. I'd done this. I was responsible.

As though she'd read my thoughts, she squeezed my shoulder and said, "This isn't your fault. If you want someone to blame, blame the Elites."

Deep down, I knew she was right, but I couldn't bring myself to let go of the guilt.

"Someone's been asking for you," she said.

I set aside my guilt and looked up at her. Someone? Who? It wasn't like I'd made many friends in Ortus. People were too afraid to approach me. Reina smirked, her square jawline expanding, and jerked her head sideways to say, *Follow me.*

She led me through the narrow passageway between countless beds and hanging curtains until we arrived at a blue curtain that looked like the rest of them—only this one had a bloody handprint on it. Slowly, Reina pulled aside the curtain, peeked inside, then nodded as if to confirm that it was safe to enter.

Reluctantly, I slipped through the crack in the curtain, and the moment I entered the tiny space, my heart nearly climbed out of my throat.

"Sadie?" I blurted.

Her eyes formed little moons as she smiled painfully my way.

"Y-y-you're alive," I said.

Under her nose was a white tube that ran along her cheeks and behind her ears. On the back of her hand was another plastic tube fastened with clear tape. The end of the tube carried a small amount of blood, but the rest of it was clear. It ran down the side of her arm, then up into a clear plastic bag filled with some sort of fluid.

"Wh-what is that?" I asked.

Sadie swallowed hard. "Called an IV. I had it once when I was a kid. See this?" She pointed at the tip stuck to the back of her hand. "It's actually a needle in my vein. And that up there is my IV bag."

I swallowed hard. A needle? In her vein? I'd never seen anything like it before. Not that it mattered. Nothing mattered right now. Nothing but Sadie. I wanted to cry, scream, and laugh all at the same time.

"I-I can't," I mumbled.

"Come here," she said.

I inched closer to her bed and she offered me her hand—the same hand that was jabbed with a needle. Without hesitating, I placed mine in hers. Her palms felt cold and clammy, but I didn't care. My throat swelled as I stared at the bloodstained bandage around her abdomen.

"I thought you were—" I tried, but my voice cut out.

She squeezed my hand. "I'm like a cockroach, Silver. Takes a lot—" She coughed, then grabbed at her bloody bandage and clenched her teeth. "Takes a lot to kill me."

"The arrow missed her vital organs," Reina said. She stood at the edge of Sadie's bed with her fingers wrapped around the metal frame, watching her like a concerned mother. "A few millimeters over, and we'd have lost her." She averted her gaze, no doubt trying to fight back tears. "Why don't you have a seat? I'll go monitor outside and make sure everything is going well."

With my foot, I pulled at the small wooden

chair behind me and sat down.

As tears slid down my cheeks, I rested my head against her arm. Using her other hand, she held my head, and we sat quietly, listening to each other breathe.

With my face muffled in her blanket, I said, "I killed him."

She twitched—maybe she'd fallen asleep and I scared her.

"Who?" she mumbled.

"The one who shot you," I said.

Smiling, she remained quiet. She must have been exhausted. So I lay my head back down and closed my eyes.

The initial jolt confused me.

My head bounced off Sadie's arm and I was pulled out of my dream. What was going on? I stiffened as the jerking movements became more violent.

Was she convulsing?

Big blue veins bulged from her crimson face and she jerked up and down, side to side, her head smashing into her pillow.

"H-h-help!" I shouted. "Sadie? Sadie!" I grabbed her arm, but it did nothing. She continued to convulse, no matter how hard I tried to pin her down.

At once, a doctor and a nurse came rushing past the curtain, its suspended hooks making a swooshing sound.

"What's going on?" I shouted.

Foam frothed out of Sadie's mouth.

"Sh-she was fine only minutes ago!" At least, it had felt like only a few minutes. I'd fallen asleep. Maybe more time had passed.

"She's seizing," the doctor said.

She then went on to mumble something else to the nurse, but I couldn't make out what they were saying. Something along the lines of *larzpam*. I'd probably heard that wrong. The nurse, a young redhead who seemed confused about what she was doing, listened to the doctor's orders and ran out of Sadie's small room. She immediately came back with gloves, a vial of liquid, and a syringe. I watched, terrified, as she filled her syringe and injected one of Sadie's tubes with it. The fluid ran down the line, all the way to her hand.

I wanted to ask them what they were giving her, but I couldn't bring myself to speak.

Within seconds, Sadie's seizure stopped.

The doctor—a middle-aged woman with creamy brown skin and short brown hair—reached for the pouch of fluid above Sadie's head, examined it, and said, "Is this all we have?"

The nurse nodded like she'd been caught

doing something wrong. She looked so young. Maybe a doctor in training? I imagined they'd brought in as many people as possible to assist in treating the wounded, even those who didn't have much experience.

The doctor's nostrils flared and she stared at her feet. "This is half the dosage she needs. With a wound like this, we can't be too careful about sepsis." When she caught me watching her, she forced a smile at me, one eye narrower than the other. At first, I thought she was squinting, but I soon realized it was simply the way her eyes were. Maybe she'd been injured as a child.

"Would you mind waiting outside?" she asked me.

She was friendly about it, despite the urgency in her tone, and I knew that whatever she had to discuss with the nurse would only make me more anxious. So I stepped out with a sinking feeling in my stomach.

What was she talking about? *Sepsis*? What medication were they low on?

"S-S-Silver?" came a croaky voice. "Is that you?"

My eyes widened at the sound.

Darby?

I followed the voice to a partially opened curtain a few beds away from Sadie's. When I peered inside, Darby's big puffy eyes met mine.

They looked more swollen than usual, and her bulbous nose was so red it looked like all of its blood vessels had burst. Next to her heart, she held something clear that looked to be about half the size of her face. What was that thing? A mask? Was that the reason for the redness on her nose?

I rushed inside. "What happened? Are you all right?"

She forced a smile, her thin cracked lips on the verge of splitting open. Rolling her eyes, she raised the clear mask and said, "Smoke inhalation. Can you blame me?" She coughed uncontrollably, placed the mask over her face, and sucked in a lungful of whatever it was giving her. Finally, she removed it and licked her lips. "Doctor said to keep the oxygen on. But look at what it's doing to me." She pointed at her face.

I pulled the curtain closed behind me.

"I'm so sorry," I said.

She waved a hand at me as if to say, *Don't worry about it.*

"This is my fault, child. I kept looking for my damn jewelry box. I refused to leave my home without it. But those two blond kids kept nagging me to get out. The boy even grabbed my arm. And then I fell, clumsy old me."

She pointed at a large gash the length of a banana on her arm. It was bound together by little black threads—*stitches*, I now knew. A dark rusty color ran all along the wound, and I couldn't tell if it was blood or something else.

"They wouldn't take no for an answer," she added.

Was she referring to Lyla and Lyson? They knew I lived with Darby—they must have gone in to save her.

"What jewelry box?" I asked.

Her lip quivered and she pulled at her fingers as if trying to grasp invisible rings. "My sister gave me a ring years ago, before she died. I placed it in a box to keep it safe, somewhere under my bed. I couldn't get to it in time."

"Your house was burning down," I said.

She nodded, on the verge of tears.

"I'm so sorry," I said.

She waved another trembling hand. "Don't be. I was foolish enough to keep it tucked away so far from reach." She sucked in a quivering breath. "Is that your friend over there? I heard you talking, and I heard her voice earlier, too."

I bit my lower lip, afraid that if I talked about it, I might become emotional. I was terrified. I'd only recently found out that Sadie was still alive. What if after all of this, she died? What if I had to relive the tragedy all over again?

Darby patted the edge of her bed, inviting me to sit.

I sat next to her, the thin mattress sinking against the metal frame.

"What happened to her?" she asked.

"Arrow wound," I said. "The doctor said something about being out of a certain medication, and how she only has half the dose she needs."

Darby's thin, uneven brows met at the center of her forehead. "So foolish, if ya ask me. They're splitting up medication, hoping that half dosages will be enough for most people. It's rubbish. Let us old farts die and let the young ones live."

My eyes bulged out. Had she been joking, or was she serious? Judging by the scowl on her face, it became obvious to me that she felt rather passionate about this. I parted my lips, prepared to tell her that surely she didn't mean that, when a tall male nurse with short wavy brown hair and a trimmed beard stepped in.

He smiled when he saw me, then approached Darby's bed with what appeared to be a vial of medicine in his fist.

"You must be Silver," he said.

He reached for Darby's IV bag. After inspecting it briefly, he pulled a syringe wrapped in clear plastic from his pocket.

"What is that?" Darby hissed at him.

He wasn't startled by her aggressive tone—he maintained his sweet composure, smiled again, and said, "Medicine."

Darby didn't seem impressed that he'd stated the obvious.

The nurse must have noticed her frustration. While unwrapping the syringe, he said, "It's an antibiotic for the wound you have on your arm. Given our living conditions, we can't be too careful."

"You're giving me an antibiotic for a simple cut? Some people have been stabbed!" Darby said.

Folds formed on her face as she aimed her big red nose at the poor nurse.

He pulled his face back, confused. "You're right, that doesn't make much sense." He reached behind him and grabbed a paper chart from the table at the end of her bed. "Sorry, my mistake. It says here you have another wound—"

Darby pulled her feet under her thin blanket, and the nurse's light brown eyes rolled toward them.

"May I?" he asked, pointing at her feet.

"It isn't worth a big fuss," she said.

Carefully, he pulled at the sheet and inspected her toes. "How long have you had those sores?"

Darby shrugged. "Can't say for sure. Been a while."

The nurse's smile returned, and he raised

the little vial of fluid at eye level. "This will help."

"I don't want it," Darby said.

The nurse—William, read his nametag— scratched the back of his neck and stared at her. "Those sores could get pretty ugly, Darby. Not to mention, that wound on your arm. If it does become infected, we won't have any antibiotics left to treat it. This will also work as a preventive measure."

Darby folded her arms over her saggy chest. "Sorry, my boy, but I don't want it. Instead, I'd like to donate my antibiotics to Silver's friend over there—Sadie." She pointed in Sadie's general direction.

William stepped toward her, his tall figure slanting down slightly. "You do understand that if the infection spreads, it could kill you, right?"

A hint of a smile pulled at Darby's lips. It was almost as if she wanted to die. "Fine by me."

William sighed, then nodded courteously. "All right. It's your decision. A very generous decision."

He glanced my way, but I was too shocked to say anything.

"I'll bring this over to the doctor now," he said.

As he slipped past the curtain, Darby stuck the mask over her face and breathed in a

270

lungful of oxygen. While blowing out, she removed the mask and turned her head toward me.

"Darby—" I said.

With a flick of her finger, she shushed me. "I'm seventy-eight years old, Silver. If the infection doesn't kill me, the smoke inhalation probably will. It would have been a waste of perfectly good medicine. Besides, I've lived my life. And to be honest, I want to see my sister again. Her, and my parents. I'm done here, in this life."

My throat swelled. How could she sacrifice herself for someone she didn't even know? I was beyond thankful for her having given Sadie the antibiotics, but I still couldn't wrap my head around her decision.

"You two have something special," she added. "It would be such a shame to take that away from you because of a lousy medicine shortage. You deserve more, my child."

"Darby, I can't—"

"You don't have to thank me," she cut me off. "I want to do this. I'm happy to."

I blinked hard, my eyes filling with tears. I couldn't believe she was willing to die to save Sadie's life.

"Thank you," I said anyway.

She smiled sweetly, her pale lips twitching, then started coughing again. I helped her place the mask over her face and stayed with her as she breathed in and out. Pulling my chair up close, I held her cold, veiny hand as her eyelids became heavy.

After a few minutes, she pulled the mask off, looking exhausted. "Why don't you go be with your friend?"

I shook my head. "Thanks to you, I'll have plenty of time for that later. Right now, I'd like to be with you."

She put the mask over her mouth again, looking more peaceful than before. And I sat there, listening to the sound of oxygen flowing through the mask, not quite understanding how this world could be so horrific yet so magnificent at the same time.

CHAPTER 24

Y ou okay?" Reina asked as she walked toward the hospital.

I wasn't sure how to answer that. The doctors couldn't give me any straight answers, and every time I tried to talk to someone, they were in too much of a hurry to look at me.

I gave Reina a one-shoulder shrug, and she joined me near the hospital entrance. Without a word, she leaned her back against the wall, same as me, and gazed out toward the back gates where the river flowed.

It was much quieter outside than it had been earlier, and the rain had stopped.

"Have the carts left yet?" I asked.

She sucked in a lungful of air as if breathing for the first time, then let it out. It almost seemed like she was sad about it. Maybe she was. After all, Ortus was no longer Ortus. Without its citizens, this village was nothing but ruins.

"They have," she said. "They'll return in a day or two to pick up more people."

Wasn't that a risk? What if we were attacked during that time? Reina must have read my thoughts. She stabbed her sword into the dirt next to her feet and leaned on it. "Don't worry about being here, Silver. A lot of people are concerned, but I guarantee you that nothing is going to happen." She pointed backward, toward the village entrance. "The entire thing collapsed. No one's coming through there."

"What about over there?" I pointed at the eastern gates, where Sadie and I had entered after floating down the river. It was a side entrance to the village—one that required a boat.

Reina scoffed. "The river? I wouldn't worry about that. If anyone is dumb enough to try to attack us from the river, they'll be swimming with the fish."

I understood what she meant. Unless someone had a large ship, it would be rather difficult to send an entire army into the village. They would have to come in small groups at a time.

"Are any Champions staying behind?" I asked.

She gazed up at the clearing sky. "A few. We have about thirty Champions willing to stay behind. The rest are moving along with everyone else."

"How do we know it's safe where they're going?"

She paused, likely thinking over scenarios.

Scratching her right eyebrow, she said, "Finn has been preparing for an evacuation for years. We hoped this day would never come, but we always felt it was something we needed to prepare for. Years ago, he sent people to a location several miles from here—a place he's been referring to as New Ortus. We have about twenty people who live there permanently, and for the last few years, they've been expanding the village.

"So a second village," I said.

"Exactly."

We stood quietly for a while as I thought about Sadie, wondering if she'd be okay. It made me sick to my stomach, and the more I thought about it, the sadder I became. Slowly, memories of Grandma crept into my mind, and all I wanted was to fall apart. I wanted her— needed her—more than ever right now. I wished I could hug her tight and have her tell me that everything would be okay.

The thought of Mother saddened me too, despite how cruel she was to me. I'd always wished that with time, she would learn to love me properly. Maybe if I'd stayed in Olympus and listened to Mr. Darwin... maybe he'd have brought Mother into Olympus, too, and for the first time since I'd known her, she might have been happy.

I pushed these thoughts away. It wasn't my responsibility to make Mother happy, even though it had always felt like it.

Then, I thought of Darby, and how any day now, she might die. In a sense, Darby had reminded me of Grandma—a sweet old woman wanting nothing more than to help those around her.

Why was everyone dying? Why was there so much death on Earth? It was cruel, and awful, and made me wish I'd never been born.

Reina patted my shoulder, preventing me from spiraling any further. "Hang in there. The doctors are doing everything they can for Sadie."

I nodded quietly, picturing Sadie's pale face against the white hospital pillow.

She'll be okay, I told myself.

I wasn't sure this was true, but I needed to keep hoping.

"How's Finn?" I asked.

"He's stable," Reina said. "But there were several fractures. It'll be a while before he's back to normal—if he ever is."

I felt sorry for Finn. He'd risked his life to save us all, and now, he was suffering because of it.

For a split second, I almost blamed myself again. I almost told myself that this was my fault and that Finn's injuries would have never happened if it wasn't for me.

But I was growing sick and tired of feeling like a bad guy—like a victim. I was sick of the guilt. Finn had made his choice. He'd allowed me to stay inside the village, knowing full well that his people may be harmed because of it. That wasn't on me. It was on him and on everyone else who'd stood by me when Finn told them I was wanted by our enemies.

I didn't blame them—I didn't want to blame anyone, including myself. It served no purpose. All it did was make me feel like garbage, and I had enough things to feel awful about already.

I sensed Reina's gaze on me.

"Are you okay?" she asked.

A gray cloud rolled by overhead, one that looked like a giant turtle. I smiled at it and said, "I'm okay. I'm tired, angry, and in pain, but I'm okay." Then, I turned sideways, my shoulder pressed up against the wall so I could face her. "Will we fight back?"

She tucked a strand of black hair behind her ear. "What do you mean?"

"The Elites," I said. "Will we fight back? You all fought to keep me here, right? I'm supposed to be some sort of symbol for hope. What does that even mean? If I'm supposed to represent freedom, then shouldn't we be fighting for it?"

Her right eyebrow popped up and she smiled at me, her chin elevated. "Is that what you want? To go to war with the Elites? With the Woodfaces?"

"I want to free my people," I said. "I want this cruelty to stop."

Her smile never fading, she said, "That's always been Finn's plan. What happened today doesn't change that. And now that we have you, that's exactly what we intend to do."

CHAPTER 25

The sound of raindrops hitting the outside patio calmed me. I drifted in and out of sleep despite being uncomfortable on the makeshift bed I'd been given. It wasn't until halfway through the night, when a loud roll of thunder shook Finn's house, that I jolted upright in a cold sweat.

A few people around me turned in their sleep, no doubt disrupted by the menacing storm. Wind howled and leaves rustled in the distance as rain splattered onto the roof.

I stared at the ceiling, willing myself back to sleep.

Around me, dozens upon dozens of people breathed—some snoring—out of synchronicity. There were so many breathing sounds that it became hard to relax. But what choice did we have? The only place that hadn't burned down, aside from the hospital, was Finn's house and the barn.

Most people had settled for sleeping in Finn's house.

Some slept on the wooden floor, while many others had made beds out of hay, clothes, or old blankets.

Despite being exhausted, I couldn't go back to sleep. Instead, I continued to recall the prior day's events—vivid flashes of blood splattering, people screaming, and Sadie collapsing to her knees. It became so real that I had to swallow several times to keep from vomiting stomach acid.

The room spun, and I sealed my eyes shut, hoping it would stop.

But it didn't. What was this? Anxiety? I needed fresh air.

I considered stepping out onto the second-story balcony—the same one Finn had brought me onto the first day I arrived in Ortus—but I was afraid that opening the door might wake people. Instead, I carefully stepped over bodies, the occasional flashes of lightning making their silhouettes visible.

When I reached the top of the staircase, a yellow glow crept up the sidewall.

Finally, I could see.

I followed the light down to the main floor and through an open door. It led me into a kitchen-style room with a circular dining table where Reina sat. She seemed to be concentrating, with her head bowed and her fingers tapping a large sheet of paper on the table.

Next to her was an oil lantern, its shiny black metal frame looking wet around the orange fire.

I stepped forward and a wooden floor panel creaked underneath me.

Reina's eyes shot up. "Storm keeping you up?"

"Yeah," I said, joining her at the table. I pulled out a chair and sat down.

The paper between us was a large map—a colorful array of blues, greens, and browns.

"What is that?" I asked. "Ortus?"

Reina smirked and pointed at a small dot at the bottom right-hand corner of the map. "That's Ortus."

"And the rest?" I asked.

Reina shrugged. "Land, all around us. This right here..." She dragged her finger across the map, but not too far. "That's New Ortus."

She tapped her index finger on the dot several times, seemingly lost in thought.

"There are no mountains," I pointed out.

Her dark, orange-hued eyes shot up at me. "In New Ortus? No, there aren't."

"Isn't that dangerous?" I asked.

She started tapping the map again, right over New Ortus. "It isn't ideal, no. But it's near water."

I followed the river that ran from Ortus, all the way up to New Ortus and even farther. I couldn't believe how much land there was around us. I hadn't imagined there to be this much.

"Why did you pick this location as a second village?" I asked.

She sighed and rubbed her grimy forehead. "It used to be a village, decades ago. When Finn found it, half of it was still intact. It seemed like the best idea at the time. What better place to migrate to than a village that's already constructed?"

But she kept tapping the map. What was she thinking about? What was she so concerned about? Was it because I'd mentioned there were no mountains? Had I pointed out how exposed we were in a place like New Ortus?

That couldn't be the reason for her anxiety. Reina was a smart woman, and Finn, a smart man. Surely, they'd already come to terms with the location's vulnerability.

"Is there a stone wall around it?"

She laughed. "No, Silver, there's no wall," she said, almost impatiently. "We *are* exposed. But that's not the problem."

"Then, what's the problem?"

Her eyes rolled up at me, the lantern's glow

causing uneven shadows to spread the right side of her face. It was as if she was trying to determine whether I should be privy to the information in her head.

She blew out some air through tight lips and dragged her finger sideways toward thick green markings that sat across a different river. A forest?

"That's Woodface territory. It used to be here." She dragged her finger across the river, right into the forest. "But Finn ordered them to relocate when the treaty was signed."

I stared at their new territory, noting how close it was to New Ortus.

"Why are they so close to us?" I asked.

She shifted her attention back onto New Ortus. "That wasn't supposed to be *us*. It was a backup plan we hoped we'd never have to act on. And at the time, the Woodfaces were our allies. We agreed to stop fighting each other."

"So they know about New Ortus?"

She rubbed her face again, this time, spreading what looked like dried blood or dirt into her black hairline.

"The information was never shared with them, but that doesn't mean we're safe."

We sat in silence for a few minutes, Reina's eyes growing larger and larger by the second. It was like she was playing scenarios in her mind, many of them terrifying her.

"So what do we do?" I asked.

This time, she rubbed her entire face with both hands. She must have been beyond exhausted. Maybe trying to come up with a plan in the middle of the night wasn't the best idea.

"I don't know," she admitted. "But I think—"

She stopped, flattened her palms across her map, and eyeballed the ceiling. "Do you hear that?"

I shifted my eyes. "Hear what?"

Then, I heard it. It was faint, especially when masked by the heavy rain, but it was there.

Horses. People. Voices.

"I thought everyone was inside," I said.

Reina stood up quickly, her wooden chair sliding behind her. "They are."

She rushed to the back door of Finn's house—one that led to a lower-level patio—and opened it wide. "The carts are back," she said in a panic. "Why are they back already?"

Although difficult to see through the curtain of falling water, I was able to make out the large carts coming through Ortus's back gates. Ahead of them was Maz, riding on her large black-and-white horse.

Everything was so dark that it was difficult to make out how many carts had returned. Had all four come back? Suddenly, a flash of lightning lit up the sky, and I saw something that made my stomach sink.

"Those carts," I said, sticking my arm out into the rain. "They're—they're full of people. Why are they still full of people?"

Reina's big eyes rolled my way.

Something was wrong.

"Come on," she said, bolting back into Finn's house.

CHAPTER 26

We ran out through the front door, and right when I stepped out onto Finn's wraparound balcony, the underneath of my bare foot slipped across the wet wood. I caught myself on the railing before falling, then had to run twice as fast to catch up to Reina.

She ran across the field and down toward the river where I had watched Penelope's body float away.

But as we descended the hill, Maz met up with us. She jumped off her horse, landing right next to Reina, and began shouting over the rain. Behind her, the carts took a turn and raced toward the barn.

I watched as men, women, and children climbed out of the carts. Some adults helped the younger children, as well as the elderly, step down into the wet grass. Everyone was soaked and probably freezing. A few thin women held on to themselves, trying to wrap their arms around their bodies for warmth.

"Burned down," Maz said. "All of it."

"Any survivors?" Reina shouted, water bounding off her flapping lips.

Maz shook her head, then jerked it sideways as if to say, *Let's finish this conversation out of the rain.*

They ran toward the barn and I followed closely, my feet splashing in the cold wet grass.

Inside, people gathered in small groups to keep one another warm. At the top corner of the barn was a large hole caused by the fire, and through it came heavy rain. Everyone kept away from that corner, some sitting on bales of hay, others leaning against the barn's interior walls.

A few pigs grunted from within their enclosures, and chickens clucked, but for the most part, the animals were quiet. I stared up at the barn's roof, thankful it hadn't collapsed. What would they have done with the animals? Left them outside until it was time to migrate them?

Maz inched closer to Reina.

"All of it. Gone," she whispered.

Reina wiped her dripping face with her wet sleeve. "All of it?"

But by the way Maz was staring at her, it was obvious that when she'd said "all of it," she wasn't exaggerating.

Reina's brows furrowed. "What are we supposed to do now?"

Her voice came out a bit louder than I'd have expected. She noticed it, too. When several eyes turned on her, she stepped toward the barn's open gates, guiding Maz away from the crowd.

"Did the Woodfaces do it?" Reina asked quietly.

Maz ran a hand through her short wet hair. "I think so. Who else would have done that? It was fresh, Reina." She made a sour face like she was smelling something awful. Had she seen dead bodies? Had they been decomposing?

"How fresh?" Reina asked.

"Last twenty-four hours," Maz said.

Reina planted her hands on her hips and stared out toward the burned village. "They aren't stopping."

Maz shook her head.

"What are we going to do now?" came a croaky voice.

Behind us, an old man and his two grandchildren approached. He stood with trembling legs as if he'd walked all day. His grandchildren—a boy and a girl—stared at Maz and Reina with huge, watery eyes. They were probably terrified beyond belief.

"We aren't sure," Reina admitted.

Voices erupted inside the barn, and more worried faces emerged from the darkness.

"What do you mean, you aren't sure?" someone said.

"We have no home!"

"We're going to die!"

The young children near us threw their little hands over their mouths and started crying.

"I don't wanna die," one of them pleaded.

Maz raised a stiff arm and shouted, "We aren't going to die! We're going to figure this out."

"How?" someone asked.

People continued to bicker back and forth. Everyone was scared. So was I. How were we supposed to survive now? The Woodfaces were still after us. It was only a matter of time before they found another way to get inside of Ortus. We couldn't stay here, but we had nowhere to go.

My heart skipped a beat as I watched Maz and Reina exchange a look that told me we were in danger.

"Finn needs to know," Reina said, walking out of the barn.

Maz nodded and followed. I jogged to keep up, while behind me, a few people did the same. Reina ran through the rain, water blasting from beneath her feet.

When we arrived at the hospital, she stuck out a flat hand that told us we weren't coming in. Although I didn't want to stand out in the freezing rain, I understood why she'd told us to stay back. The last thing the hospital needed was more bodies filling their already crowded space.

Everyone else—about a dozen of us—waited outside. Some people continued to argue, their panicked voices muffled by the loud storm.

I expected Reina to return with a plan, but was surprised when Finn was the one to push the door open. He limped his way out, a faint yellow light behind him darkening his silhouette. He looked tired. Under his eyes were deep blue bags—the kind someone gets when they haven't slept for days.

He looked skinnier, too. Maybe it was because of the slack blue robe he was wearing. Over his thigh was a big bloodstain. Was it seeping through? Was this why he was limping? Around his neck was a sling like the one he'd worn earlier that day, only this one appeared much cleaner and better secured. He limped, holding himself up with his wooden staff.

No one said anything. What was there to say? This bruised and beaten man had risked his life to save all of us. We owed him everything. As he stepped out, he jabbed his staff into the dirt and everyone bowed their heads.

"Reina tells me New Ortus was destroyed," he said, matter-of-factly.

I admired that about Finn. He said it like it was. He didn't play games or try to downplay anything. No wonder everyone loved him.

No one said anything until finally, Maz cleared her throat. "Yes, sir, all of it. There were no survivors."

Finn regripped his staff, then rested his forehead against the top part. I could tell the news hurt him deeply.

"What do we do now?" someone asked.

I wasn't sure who had spoken.

Finn gazed at the crowd, his stare blank. Lightning snapped overhead and I flinched when explosive thunder shook the ground.

"We can't stay here," Finn said.

Everyone looked at each other as if he'd spoken a different language.

"I know we have nowhere to go," he continued. "But if we stay here, we'll die."

Voices loudened as people started arguing.

"That's a huge risk!"

"We could die out there!"

"Or be massacred," came a grim voice. "Like everyone in New Ortus."

"Enough," Reina said. She stood tall next to

Finn, scowling. "Finn's right. They've already attacked New Ortus, which means they're searching the lands. It's only a matter of time before they find our back door."

Finn sighed, his shoulders deflating. "It's a gamble, I know. But we don't have any other choice. We can head west, past New Ortus, and search for a safe location."

"Search for a location?" someone asked. The woman stepped forward, then hesitated when everyone's focus shifted onto her. She rubbed at her wet throat, something that looked like a nervous tic. "We have young children, and injured people." She pointed a thumb at Ortus's back wall. "How are we supposed to get everyone out of Ortus? And how will we gather more food if we're traveling?"

"We have a map of these lands," Finn said. He turned to Reina, who nodded to confirm. "We can study the map and locate the area we feel would be safest for our people. Somewhere near mountains or a forest. Somewhere secluded where the Woodfaces won't find us."

"Won't find us?" a man said. "You said so yourself: they're looking for us. They could be miles away from here, waiting for us to emerge. Maybe we should stay inside these walls and prepare to fight back."

Finn shook his head. "Even if we manage to defeat the Woodfaces, the Elites won't stop. They'll find another clan and send them after us. This won't end." He paused. "We have excellent archers here in Ortus. If we're attacked out in an open field, I welcome it."

A moment of silence weighed on us.

"Today, we were surprised," he continued. "We were attacked and we weren't prepared. As we travel, we'll be prepared. We'll bring all of our arrows and I promise you, if the Woodfaces are foolish enough to strike again, they will lose their army."

Most of the men nodded, some of them pumping their fists, while one woman—the same timid lady who'd questioned Finn on his plan—scratched at her neck again and squeezed her arms around her belly. It was obvious she was scared. Why wouldn't she be? After today, the last thing we wanted was more violence. But Finn's plan made sense. If we were prepared for an attack, we had much better odds of coming out victorious.

"Come on," Finn said, stepping away from the hospital.

Reina reached for him, likely wanting to tell him to get back inside the hospital, but he pulled away.

Jabbing his staff in the grass, he led us all to his house, where Reina's oil lantern still lit up the lower level. This time, he didn't refuse when Reina offered to help him climb the stairs.

It was sad to see.

Everyone slowed down, climbing one step at a time as Finn struggled to make his way to the top. He eventually entered, and everyone followed. Our voices and footsteps shook the house, and I wondered how long it would be before everyone upstairs woke up.

Maybe the storm would mask the noise we were making.

Reina led Finn into his kitchen and pulled out a chair for him. He sat down, nearly falling over, and set his staff against a white paneled wall next to him.

"This is us—" he said, pointing at Ortus.

Water dripped down his finger, soaking the entire village.

Reina pulled open a drawer, took out a cloth, and handed it to Finn. He wiped his hands, his neck, his face, then came back to the map.

Everyone leaned in, wanting to see, but Reina ordered them to take a step back.

"This is the only map we have," she growled.

The drawings were so intricate—so well-defined. The map had no doubt been created using a machine. No wonder Reina felt so protective of it. No way could she replicate this map—at least not without Elite technology.

Finn hovered over the map for some time as if trying to draw a line with his mind.

He tapped his finger on a forest that ran along the river—the same river next to Ortus. "We'd be safest within these woods," he said.

"Would we?" Reina said. "The Woodfaces seem to have a thing for fire."

Finn sighed, his nostrils doubling in size.

Reina wasn't wrong.

Maz stepped forward and leaned over Finn's shoulder. "What about there?" She pointed across the river, where the map ended.

Finn raised an eyebrow but didn't say anything.

"We don't know what lies beyond the map," Reina said.

"Well, we won't know until we try," Maz argued.

"Is that how you want to approach this?" Reina said. "You want to gamble with the lives of our people—"

"Enough," Finn ordered, and Reina retreated into herself. "Of course no one wants to take a gamble, but what do you propose we do? We thought New Ortus would save us, and here we are. There are no bad ideas here. Maz isn't wrong to think that maybe we could cross the river and build a home farther away."

Reina leaned forward, her shoulders slouched like she was trying to block her voice from the rest of us. "What if the stories are true, Finn?"

Finn shook his head. "Those stories are preposterous. The Earth isn't flat, and our ancestors knew this. These stories were made up by the Elites to deter the slaves from trying to run."

What were they talking about?

When Finn caught me staring curiously, he said, "Haven't you been told this story, Silver?"

"What story?" I said.

"About how Lutum and its surrounding lands were all that was left of the world. About how our science books and geography—"

"We didn't have many geography books in Lutum," I said.

"Exactly," he said. "The Elites want you to believe that this"—he jabbed his finger at the center of the map—"is all that's left of the world."

I knew what he was talking about. Such stories had circulated throughout Division 9 when I was a child.

"The pits," I said.

He smiled. "Is that what you called it?"

I nodded. "That's what my mother called it. She said if I didn't behave, she'd walk me to the ends of Earth's remains and throw me into the pits. I was always told the Earth was flat and that we were the only piece left."

"I've never heard that," someone mumbled next to me.

"Me neither."

"It was a scare tactic for the people of Lutum," Finn said loudly. "It isn't true."

I didn't understand. How could it not be true? It was what I'd been taught my whole life.

Reina looked embarrassed for having brought it up and made it a point to break eye contact with us.

"Don't be embarrassed," Finn said. "Many people believe the story. After all, we haven't been able to locate maps of anywhere else. It seems plausible."

The sound of wood creaking echoed behind us and everyone turned to look. One by one, a few people entered the kitchen with puffy red eyes and gaping mouths as they yawned.

"Did we wake you?" Finn said.

A few people shrugged.

"We were discussing our next course of action," Finn said. "New Ortus is no longer an option."

The second people started raising their voices, Finn pointed at the ceiling. "Please, keep it down. Those who need rest should be allowed to get it."

The kitchen became crowded and hot,

though it was something I welcomed after being soaked from head to toe.

"We were discussing where we should relocate to next," Finn said.

A few yawning people tried to squeeze closer to get a good look at the map.

A short old man—someone who had been with us since the hospital—raised a stubby, black-nailed finger like he was asking for permission to speak.

Finn smiled at him. It astonished me how despite the tremendous amount of pain he was in, Finn still managed to be polite with his people.

"I, um, you said there ain't no bad ideas," the man said.

He was short, plump, and had half a head of white hair. The rest was bald.

He pointed at the map. "May I?"

People moved aside to allow the old man through. He walked with a limp, holding on to the backs of chairs for support, until he reached Finn's side. With a heavy breath I imagined smelled like rotten fish, he leaned forward, his gray eyes narrowing at the map.

"Well, I'll be," he said.

"What is it?" Finn asked.

The man pointed at the corner of the map, right near the edge of it. "See that?"

Finn inched closer, but he looked puzzled.

"What am I looking at?"

"The text," he said.

At the top right corner of the map were a few letters on an angle. But the corner of the map was missing, as if someone had held on too tightly while trying to keep it out of someone else's hands.

"Port W—" Finn said. "I've never seen the rest of the map."

"Port Williamson," the man said. "My pop trained dere for da military." He jabbed his finger hard on the W. "Underground bunker over dere."

Finn's eyes widened, as did Reina's and Maz's.

"Underground?" Finn said. "Are there people still living there?"

"Oh, I wouldn't think so," the old man said. "Pop said da place was abandoned during the war."

Finn turned in his chair and reached for the man's shoulder. "Do you know anything else—"

"Clayson," the man said, patting his chest.

"Clayson," Finn said. "Do you know anything else about this bunker? Entry points? Are they electronic, or manual? Is there a security system in place?"

Clayson's eyes went big as if Finn was asking him to start counting backward from a thousand.

"Oh, I don't know none o' dat," he said. "My old man told me 'bout it. He always said it sat right on de edge of Port Williamson."

"Which edge?" Reina asked.

The man shrugged, looking clueless.

Finn rubbed his face and sighed. "We have to try. If we—"

"But it's across the river," Reina said. "How are we supposed to get our livestock across?"

"Oh, dat's easy," Clayson said. He dragged his thick finger near the letters of Port Williamson and pointed at a narrow line that ran across the river. "Dere's a bridge, right dere."

A hint of a smile pulled at Finn's bruised lips. He locked eyes with Reina, until after a beat, he said, "We leave at dawn."

CHAPTER 27

Sadie cracked her eyes open and licked her dry, flaking lips.

She searched the ceiling and blinked hard, looking disoriented. Had they given her more medication?

"Wh-what's going on?" she moaned.

Through the hospital windows came a peach-colored glow, which told me we would soon be leaving.

"We're leaving," I said.

Her bright eyes bulged and she tried to sit up, but I placed a hand over her collarbone. "No, it's okay. They're setting up the carts to make them comfortable for the injured. You'll be on there."

She blinked hard again, crust sticking to her eyelashes. "What are you talking about?" She wiped her mouth and looked around her as if she'd heard a mouse.

"I know you're confused," I said. "But Finn

has this all under control."

"Finn," she breathed.

"He's alive," I confirmed.

I knew she wanted to hear it.

"Wh-what about—" she tried.

"New Ortus," I said. "It's been destroyed. There's nothing left."

"Then why are we rushing to leave?" she said.

"Because it's only a matter of time before the Woodfaces find their way inside again."

She breathed out, her breath sour. But I didn't mind it. Bad smells were something I'd been around my entire life. Besides, I enjoyed being next to Sadie; the rest didn't matter.

"Attention, please," came a voice from behind the curtain. "We will be transporting everyone out one at a time. I ask that you remain calm—"

"This is ridiculous," Sadie said. "I can walk out—" She tried to sit up again, but winced in pain and lay back down.

"You need to rest," I said.

It was obvious that the last thing she wanted to do was rest. But her puncture wound was deep, and she needed to give her body enough time to recover.

"I wanted to let you know what was going on. I'll see you out there, okay?"

She nodded, and just as I went to turn away,

she grabbed my hand. Despite being clammy, her touch was warm and soft and made me feel secure. She quietly held on for several seconds before saying, "Be safe."

I forced a smile and left the hospital as medics scrambled to transport patients out from their rooms and into the carts outside. The setup wasn't perfect—many people cried out as they were lifted and placed onto makeshift stretchers. But what choice did we have? If these people weren't transported in the carts, they'd be left behind and risked being burned alive by our enemies.

A little bit of pain now was better than getting killed.

When I stepped outside, I filled my lungs with thick, humid air. The rain had stopped, and now a thin layer of fog licked at people's ankles.

"You just gonna stand there?" came Lyson's voice.

He smiled at me, his light blond hair waving in the wind. I wasn't sure what he was talking about. It wasn't like anyone needed my help.

"Finn gave us a new order," he said, pointing toward the barn. "We need to empty the carts of their food and supplies by half."

I gasped. "By half? You mean we're leaving half our food supply behind?"

He shrugged. "We have to. We only have

four carts—two for supplies and two for people. But now that we're filling one of them with the sick and injured, along with tons of medical supplies, that would only leave one cart for the children and the elderly. It's not enough. Not everyone can walk over a hundred miles."

"But what if we run out—" I said.

Right then, Reina's loud voice made me flinch. "Finn's orders, Silver! I don't care what you do—make yourself useful."

I decided to follow Lyson to the barn. It was difficult to watch people climb in and out of the supply cart, only to remove large bags of wheat, beans, vegetables, and more. By the time everyone was done, the cart only held essential supplies for our people and our livestock.

Lyla was the last one to hop out of the cart and throw a bag of carrots into Lyson's arms. She wiped her glistening forehead, then grabbed her long blond hair and tied it up into a high ponytail. Panting, she said, "Don't worry so much, Silver."

"Worry?" I said. "I'm not—"

She laughed. "It's all over your face. You think we're gonna starve."

Wasn't it reasonable to think that? Having grown up in Lutum, I knew how much food was needed to keep a population alive. The food we

306

had piled up in our cart would only last us a week, if that. We relied heavily on our crops. How would we cultivate more food once we arrived at our new home? How did we know the ground—the soil—would be suitable for agriculture?

I reminded myself that these people—those responsible for gardening—were like Grandma and me. They had experience growing food, which meant they knew what they were doing. Good chance they had already stored and packed countless seeds for planting.

But plant growth took time. It didn't take a week—it took months before vegetables could be harvested. What would we do until then?

Slowly, my focus shifted onto the five cows and two bulls lined up next to the cart. Then, pigs snorted, and I stared at their large round bellies.

"We aren't going to wipe out our livestock," Lyla said, apparently noticing my anxiety. "It's called *hunting*."

She rolled her eyes and huffed as if I were asking her to bring me eggs and bacon on a golden plate. It was like a part of her couldn't stand being around me, and I didn't understand why.

"Lyla, give her a break," Lyson said. "We've never been close to starving—" He paused, watching me. "It's a reasonable fear."

I hadn't given much thought to my anxiety up until that moment. In Lutum, I'd missed several meals because of food shortages. It wasn't uncommon to go a few days without eating. I supposed now that I'd escaped Lutum, I didn't want to be reminded of its living conditions. On several occasions, I'd given Grandma my portion because she'd become skin and bone, and I was afraid that she'd collapse and break something.

The elderly who could no longer produce were often taken away and never brought back.

No one knew where they went, but I didn't want Grandma to leave.

Lyson brought the bag of carrots to a pile next to the barn. It was an awful thing to look at—all that food, all those supplies, that would simply go to waste.

"Maybe if we find someplace safe, we'll come back for the food," he said, no doubt sensing my emotions.

I didn't respond.

It wasn't long before everyone had finished preparing for the migration. People gathered around the carts, our Champions armed from head to toe and prepared to defend us.

I stood next to the hospital cart as they loaded Sadie on. She appeared pale and weak, and despite being bounced around on a gurney, she looked like she was on the verge of falling asleep. I wished I could go up there with her, but space was already limited. So I stood quietly, waiting for us to depart.

It wasn't until the carts were full that I realized something.

"Where's Darby?" I asked.

A few heads turned my way, but no one seemed to know who I was talking about.

"Darby," I repeated. "She was in the hospital."

A warm hand touched my shoulder, and I spun around to find the nurse from earlier—William—standing tall behind me. He smiled sweetly at me, rubbed my back, and said, "She's still in the hospital."

My eyes went big. "What? Why? There's still space." I pointed at the cart.

William rubbed his fuzzy brown beard, almost like he was uncomfortable. "It isn't about the space. It was her decision."

"But—"

"I'm sorry," he said, looking genuinely sad.

He helped another old man climb the ramp up to the cart, its weathered gray wood cracking under the man's feet.

Without thinking, I darted toward the hospital. About halfway there, Reina met me from the opposite direction with Finn leaning against her, his arm around her shoulder for support.

"Where are you going?" she asked. "We're leaving in a few minutes."

"My friend," I said. "She's still inside—"

"Darby," Finn said. He chewed on his bottom lip. "I tried, Silver. I really did. She doesn't want to travel. She said it'll be too hard on her."

Only then did I remember her sun allergy. If she rode with us, she would suffer.

I played out various scenarios in my head. What if we lay a blanket over her? Wouldn't that work? We could keep her skin away from the sun.

Finn pulled away from Reina, using his good hand to control his staff. He limped toward me as I stared wide-eyed at nothing, trying to come up with a solution. His large, comforting hand took me by surprise.

He gave my shoulder a little squeeze. "You should go say goodbye before we leave."

Without responding, I ran to the hospital and rushed inside. Most beds were now empty, and many curtains hung open, revealing even more empty beds. Wooden carts sat all over the place, most of them without supplies. Everything felt so bare.

A few moans slipped through closed curtains, and someone laughed.

"Ain't this the way to go," came a croaky

voice.

"At least we'll be warm," someone else said.

"I'm ready."

"Me, too."

How many people had stayed behind? I stormed through the large room, straight for Darby's bed. When I pulled the curtain open, her tired, puffy eyes rolled up at me. Around her nose and mouth was a thick red line— markings left behind by the mask she was wearing earlier.

But the mask wasn't there anymore, and neither were the oxygen tanks.

"Where's your mask?" I asked. "And the oxygen?"

Her lip twitched. "They took it. Do you have any idea how useful something like that is?"

I clenched my jaw. "Took it? But you need it!"

She didn't seem to care, at least not as much as I did. With flat eyelids, she shook her head from side to side. "I don't need it, Silver. I told them to take it. I'm ready. I want to go. Someone else will need it more than me."

I hurried to the side of her bed, my throat swelling.

Why wasn't she even trying? Wasn't life worth fighting for?

She raised a fist, her fingers curled downward, and shook it. I wasn't sure what she was doing, but I got the feeling she was trying to give me something.

"What is it?" I asked.

She shook her fist again, so I placed my palm underneath.

Finally, she loosened her fingers and a small silver ring fell into my palm. It was warm, shiny, and had a small engraving on the inside. I brought it up to my eye and squinted.

"L," I said. "What does it stand for?"

She smiled at the high, wooden ceiling as if looking at something beautiful, like mountains.

"Lillian," she breathed. "My sister."

"It's beautiful," I said, handing it back to her.

She gently pushed my hand away. "No, I want you to have it."

"What?" I exclaimed. "Why would I keep something like this? It's yours. I can't take it."

"I want you to," she said. "Keep it as a reminder for me, will you? I want you to remember that the only thing that matters in this life is love. Friends, family. That's all." She coughed, blood sprinkling onto her veiny hand this time. She wiped it clean with the thin sheet over her. "Nothing else matters, you hear me?"

I nodded.

The ring felt hot in my palm. I stared at it as an overhead light flashed, causing the ring to sparkle.

"Does it fit?" she asked.

I hesitated but then tried sliding it on each finger. It wasn't until I reached my third finger on my right hand that it slipped on snuggly.

I'd never worn jewelry before. I stuck my hand out, admiring how shiny it was. But it still didn't feel right. This wasn't mine.

"It's a gift," Darby said, likely sensing my discomfort. "Have you ever received a gift before?"

I tried to think back to my childhood. Grandma had given me books to read, and one time, a flower for Selection Day. But I'd never received anything like this. I'd never even seen jewelry until I entered Olympus. If the Elites had caught anyone wearing jewelry, they'd have probably cut off their hand—or head.

"I, um..."

"It's okay," she said. "When someone gives you a gift, it's because they want you to have it. It makes people happy to give things."

I thought back to the time I'd made a little bunny out of clay for Grandma. The look on her face had warmed my heart so much that the next day, I collected more clay to make another animal. That evening, Mother crushed my creation with the heel of her foot and said if she ever caught me using my stupid imagination again, she'd bring me to the Defenders herself.

But I'd always held on to that memory—how excited I'd been to show Grandma her new surprise.

"Thank you," I said, rubbing the ring over and over again.

Darby laid her head back down and breathed out slowly. "You're very welcome. Now go on. Reina said everyone was leaving."

I wasn't sure whether to thank her again, touch her hand, or hug her. So I stood there, fidgeting.

"Come here," she said.

I leaned over her bed and wrapped my arms around her shoulders. She felt cold, bony, and frail, but I didn't mind. She tried to squeeze me, but she was so weak that I barely felt it, so I squeezed back.

"You be good now, you hear me?" she said. "You'll make a real difference in this world. I know it."

Her words reminded me of Grandma, and I was so thankful to have met Darby. Although I didn't want to leave, people would become upset with me for causing a delay.

"Thank you for everything," I said.

She smiled at me, then closed her eyes as if preparing to go back to sleep.

I left with a painful tightness in my throat and ran toward the carts just as the back gates were opening.

"Grab a weapon," Reina said as I approached. "And stay in rank."

CHAPTER 28

Sadie woke up, her head bouncing upright every time we hit a bump. She sat next to a large, broad-shouldered man who looked like a Champion. He inspected the foggy, open fields with a narrowed gaze as if trying to spot enemies miles away.

I wondered what had happened to him. He seemed okay from the shoulders up. Maybe his legs had been injured.

Sadie blinked hard, then craned her neck to peek at me over the cart's wooden side. "You okay down there?"

I showed her my spear as a way of saying, *I'm good.*

"Wish I could hold one of those right now," she said.

Even though she wanted to carry a weapon, she probably couldn't have managed it. Her eyelids were flat and heavy-looking, and her skin was as pale as the clouds above our heads. She still needed time to heal.

Now and then, her head disappeared, or at least most of it. A few strands of dark hair stuck out near the large Champion's shoulder, which she used as a pillow. It was sweet to see how still he sat, working hard to keep her head from rolling off.

We walked along the river's bend, the scent of freshwater making my mouth go dry. It wasn't until we'd traveled several miles that Finn allowed us to take a break—to drink from the river. He came around the row of carts and livestock, riding on a beige horse. I wasn't sure how he managed to ride so well with one arm still in his sling, but he did.

"Let us take a few minutes," he said. "Go on, have a drink. Rest your legs. If anyone needs to rotate, now is the time."

People gathered near the river's edge, lowering themselves onto their hands and knees. Some even splashed water across their sweaty faces to cool down.

I followed the crowd, and Lyson followed me.

"How you holding up?" he asked.

I shrugged, not knowing how to respond.

He knelt next to me and dipped his hands in the dark water.

I did the same, and his eyes caught my ring.

"Hey, isn't that—" he said.

"Darby's," I said. "She gave it to me."

He smiled proudly like he'd accomplished something great. "I'm glad it went to someone worthy."

I remembered Darby telling me about how Lyson and his sister had been the ones to drag her out of her home—to save her life.

"Are you the one who found it?" I asked.

He splashed water all over his face, beads dripping down his neck, and nodded. "Yeah, it was far under her bed."

I scooped up water with both hands and sipped on it. It was cold and refreshing, so I took another handful. Once my throat was coated and no longer dry, I said, "Thank you. It meant a lot to her."

A loud splash caught my attention, and laughter erupted around us. Out from the water's rippled surface came a head with a dark, patchy beard and big surprised eyes. Another man pointed at him, chuckling, then helped him back up onto land.

"What'd'ya do that for?" said the wet man.

He came out, looking scrawny with his clothes stuck to his slender body.

His friend patted him on the back, causing water to splash off him. "You looked like you needed to cool off."

The drenched man bent forward and

picked up a bow from out of the grass. He didn't seem too impressed by his friend's prank.

The laughter slowed down, and people returned to the carts. A few jumped on, while others jumped off, stretching their legs, and it wasn't long before we started moving again.

By the afternoon, the sun sat high in the sky, surrounded by only a few puffy white clouds. I was thankful for the clear weather. I couldn't imagine traveling long distances in a storm. A few dark clouds hovered in the distance, but they didn't look too worrisome.

As the carts and the livestock moved, they flattened the long grass for the rest of us, making our trek a bit easier. Every few seconds, someone swatted the air or their skin to fight the bugs. It wasn't pleasant, but I'd dealt with much worse.

By the afternoon, we came up to a forest full of fat, bushy trees. I couldn't tell what they were, but they didn't have leaves. Instead, they had strange-looking needles on their branches. I'd never seen anything like it.

"Those are called spruces," a woman said to her young boy.

The child hopped up and down with excitement and pointed at the trees. "Thpruthes!"

The forest started right along the edge of

the river and expanded sideways, making it impossible for us to continue following the river. We would have to move out into the field. As we slowed, people began asking questions.

"Are we lost?"

"We can't go in there! The carts won't fit!"

Reina came trotting next to the carts, announcing the same message over and over again, ensuring that everyone heard it.

"We will travel around the forest and reunite with the river after."

The message was repeated by others until it reached the far back of the line. Slowly, the horses turned left, and we changed our course. A few cows mooed like they were annoyed at having to make a turn. The chickens, on the other hand, hadn't stopped clucking since we left. They were distraught at having to travel, which was why we'd caged them and placed them into one of the carts.

As we traveled alongside the forest, I couldn't help but stare through the trees, wondering what sort of creatures lived within the darkness.

Were there wolves? Bears? What if one came out and attacked us? I realized this thought was silly. There were far too many of us. The sound of our footsteps and voices would probably scare them off. At least, I hoped that wild animals were afraid of large groups. I didn't know for certain, but if I'd been a wild animal, I wouldn't attempt an attack on a large group of people.

The forest grew denser and denser, and I wondered if we'd ever make it back to the river. What if this route led us somewhere else?

Suddenly, horses neighed up ahead, and screams filled the sky. The carts stopped abruptly, and panic spread through the crowd as people prepared their weapons. What was going on? Had something happened? Why weren't we moving?

Strange voices came from up ahead. I ran sideways to see beyond the carts, and that's when I spotted them: men dressed in camouflage clothing and black-painted faces. They held on to large, metal weapons with both hands and pointed them at Finn, Reina, and anyone else who dared step too close.

What were they holding? Guns? I'd read about them in history books, but I'd never seen one in person.

"What's going on?" Sadie said.

I shook my head as a way of saying, *Keep quiet.*

Carefully, I moved forward, gripping my spear.

There were four men, or at least, four that I could see. They spoke with Finn and Reina, who were no longer mounted on their horses, and jabbed their weapons at them menacingly. Reina raised both hands to her face. She was trying to tell them something, but they weren't listening. Finally, the man closest to her swung his weapon sideways as if giving her permission to do whatever it was she was asking.

Around me, tension grew. Champions looked at each other, trying to figure out whether to attack or sit still. But we couldn't just sit around. What if these men hurt people? Everyone fidgeted, some twirling their weapons in their hands, others preparing their bows.

And right when the Champions prepared to charge forward, Reina came running toward us, waving her hands over her head.

"Stand down! Stand down!" she shouted.

Stand down? Why was she telling us to stand down?

Several Champions lowered their bows, but others held on to their swords and spears.

"What's going on?" one man growled. "Why aren't we protecting our people?"

Champions gathered around Reina near the back of the carts. "You don't understand. They have machine guns. Please, stand down. If any of you try anything, we'll all be killed."

Children started sobbing, digging their faces into their parents' arms. Champions stared at each other, frozen in fear. I searched the crowd, hoping I wasn't the only one who didn't know what a machine gun was. I'd read about rifles and pistols only.

"Put your weapons on the ground," Reina ordered.

"Can't we at least try?" I said.

"Silver, now!" she snapped.

Slowly, everyone lowered their weapons.

Reina's narrow eyes darted toward the forest. I followed her gaze to where a dozen or so men hid next to the trees. They pointed their weapons at us, waiting quietly.

I didn't know what a machine gun was, but they must have been extremely dangerous if Reina felt that surrendering was the safest option for our people.

"All right!" came a loud, obnoxious voice. "Listen up, people! We ain't gonna take up too much of your time. So long as you cooperate, this exchange don't gotta be difficult." The man spoke with an accent I'd never heard before.

"On the ground, all of you," he shouted. As he walked toward the back, he pointed his gun all around, ordering people onto their bellies.

Long grass blades wiggled as people dropped down, disappearing into the grass. "If you're smart, you won't try nothin'. See we got folks hidin' in the forest right over there." He pointed his gun at the forest. "And in case y'all aren't familiar with MG 42s, they can fire sixteen thousand bullets per minute. That means y'all be dead before you even killed one of us."

I swallowed hard. I was familiar with the term *bullets*—they'd killed millions of people during the war.

A few dogs growled and barked in the distance, and the man's hateful gaze shot up toward them. I was afraid that if they didn't stay quiet, he'd shoot them. I hoped Maz had them under control.

One Champion must have lifted his head from the ground. The man with the big gun marched over to him, aimed his gun, and shouted, "Don't try to be a hero, asshole!"

He then kicked him and the man grunted.

"Now, y'all willin' to share, right? 'Cause me and my boys here haven't eaten in a few days."

He whistled, and some of the men at the front came around.

"Rest of you, get down!" shouted the leader.

I caught Sadie's terrified gaze before dropping to my knees. Slowly, I did as I'd been told and lowered myself onto my stomach. From the ground, it was difficult to see anything. Long blades of grass stood tall all around me, but every few seconds, a gust of wind parted the blades and I caught a glimpse of our enemies.

The other gunned men jumped up onto the sides of the carts and peeked inside. Children cried as the men came close to them, and a few women screamed.

"You ain't got no reason to be scared," the leader said. "Alls we want is a bit o' food, that's all."

He ran a hand over his shaved head and through his short black beard, smiling at his men as they searched the carts. He seemed thick and capable of defending himself without a weapon. Although he wasn't any larger than Finn, he had this soulless look in his dark eyes that gave me a sickening feeling—one that told me he enjoyed getting blood on his hands.

As much as I wanted to grab my spear and throw it at him, I wasn't prepared to risk the lives of everyone around me. Reina was right— we didn't stand a chance. All we could do was hope they wouldn't hurt us.

"Over here!" shouted one of his men, jabbing his gun toward the sky.

The leader's smile vanished and he jumped up onto the cart's side. It shook under his weight and creaked when he leaned over the edge. "Well, looky here. Boys, think we won ourselves the jackpot!"

The men cheered and waved their guns. It was a metallic sound that made me wince.

"You, get out," the leader said.

I wasn't sure who he was talking to until the man leading the cart let go of the horse's reins and stepped down into the grass with both hands up in the air. "Please, don't shoot. Please. I got—I got a family. A little girl. Please, I beg—"

"Shut your trap," the leader growled.

With the back of his gun, he smashed the man right in the jaw. The sound was awful—hard impact mixed with a disturbing click. The injured man collapsed to the ground, unconscious, and from the distance came more cries and sobbing.

Loud shushing sounds immediately followed as the adults tried to get the children to stay quiet.

On either side of me, a few Champions shared looks—ones that translated to, *Should we try something*?

Surprisingly, they were staring at me. Were they waiting for me to answer? It wasn't like I'd proven myself to be some great warrior. Maybe they looked to me because they thought I had more experience with people like this.

In a sense, I did—the Defenders. You couldn't rationalize with them, and if you disobeyed, they either beat you, took you away, or obliterated you. I shook my head to say, No, *don't do anything.*

As I lay there, my heart pounding hard against the soil underneath me, I thought back to Lutum. Why hadn't we tried to fight for our rights? The Defenders didn't have machine guns. They may have had weapons capable of killing someone, but if we'd planned it right, we could have taken them down with minimal deaths.

I supposed the people of Lutum had been conditioned to be afraid.

These Champions, on the other hand, had been trained to run toward danger. I couldn't compare the two.

The leader whistled again, and this time, the men hiding in the forest emerged. I saw them in fragments as the grass shielded them from view. Their footsteps, however, pounded hard as they ran toward the food cart and jumped on. They stumbled awkwardly over the bags and boxes of our food supply, laughing as they fell into each other.

The leader did the same, only he stood at the very back, watching all of us with his white knuckles around his gun. He then swayed his weapon from side to side, making a point to aim it at as many people as possible.

"I'd like to thank y'all for your hospitality," he said, and it looked like he was on the verge of laughing. Then, with a deep and rumbly voice, he shouted, "Let's go!" and the cart started moving.

He stood with his chest puffed out and his

big black boots flat against the old gray wood under him. His jaw muscles popped as he watched us. It was almost like he *hoped* one of us would stand so he could play with his gun.

"Everyone, stay down," Reina growled.

No one argued.

These weren't Woodfaces carrying bows and spears equal to ours. This was some sort of gang that had somehow collected old military gear used in the war.

All we could do was wait for them to leave.

The man standing at the edge of the cart became smaller and smaller as they drove off into the field. Finally, they descended a hill, and the man slowly disappeared, along with our entire reserve of food.

CHAPTER 29

It wasn't until they were out of sight that everyone started lamenting. Children shrieked and cried, throwing themselves into their parents' arms.

Champions got up, some grabbing their weapons out of anger, others balling their fists. People paced everywhere, not knowing what to do with themselves.

"Everyone, calm down," Reina called out.

"Calm down?" one man snapped. Veins bulged from his throat and temples as he puffed his chest out at Reina. "We lost all of our food! And you're telling us to calm down? We have little mouths to feed! And we need feeding ourselves if you expect us to stand a chance against the Woodfaces! If they attack us now–"

"If they attack us now," Reina cut him off, "we'll fight."

"And what about tomorrow?" the man said. "Huh? What about after tomorrow? After we haven't eaten in days? You think we'll be in any shape to fight?"

"He's right," said a woman gripping a longbow.

"We can hunt," someone else said.

"Don't even try that positive bullshit!" the angry man shouted.

"Whoa, now, now," came Arahm's voice. His children circled around him. "This young man has a point. We can easily feed all of our people with one deer."

The angry man scoffed. "What? One bite each? Come on, that's not true and you know it."

"We can ration," Arahm said. "And there may be fruit in that forest—"

"In *that* forest?" the angry man said. "In a spruce forest. Right. I bet we'll find plenty of fruit in there." His eyes narrowed, and he took a step toward Arahm with clenched fists as if preparing to break his nose." Are you blind or something, old man?"

Arahm didn't flinch or step back. He remained as calm as he always was and turned his attention away from the man.

"That's enough," Reina said. "Mileson, stand down."

The fuming man, Mileson, grabbed handfuls of his short curly locks and paced in circles.

330

The air around us felt hot and intense. There were so many emotions floating around that I could almost *feel* what everyone else was feeling in addition to my anxieties.

I looked around at our three remaining carts, our livestock, and our horses.

"It could be worse," I said.

Several eyes turned on me—some hateful, others curious.

"What do you mean?" someone asked.

"I mean, we're all alive, aren't we?" I paused, gauging everyone's reaction. No one responded, and it was almost like they wanted to hear what I had to say—what the *Girl Who Refused Immortality* thought. So, I continued. "They didn't kill anyone. They only took one cart. We still have all our animals, including our horses. You all saw that group. There were over a dozen men. They could have easily taken half our horses."

A few nods spread through the quickly growing crowd and one of Maz's dogs barked like it was agreeing with me. Those sitting in the cart began to climb down, wanting to hear what the conversation was about.

Then, I realized something else.

I pointed at the last cart—the one carrying Sadie, along with other injured people, and all our medical supplies. "They didn't touch our medical equipment."

"That's because we hid it," Sadie said, still sitting in the cart. She leaned over the edge, resting her chin on the wall. "All of us. We slid what we could under our feet."

Sighs of relief spread through the field.

A few injured people stood up, some limping, others blinking hard with heavy eyes.

"That's right," said an old man. He seemed bald, but when a gust of wind swept through, a few strands of hair stood up straight. He shook a finger in the air, and I couldn't tell if he was shaking it wildly on purpose, or if he was trembling. "We weren't lettin' them get anywhere near this stuff."

I shot Reina a glance. She smiled at me.

"They didn't touch our clothes, or other supplies, either," someone pointed out.

"Exactly," I said. "We have more here than I ever had in Lutum."

Several people looked away from me, likely not knowing how to respond. Others nodded, probably realizing how fortunate we really were.

"So let's keep moving," I said. "We'll figure it out as we go. Right now, we need to find shelter."

I hadn't meant to make it sound like an order, but people listened. Men, women, and children nodded, picked up their things, and started moving forward.

Reina watched me with a look that said, *Well done.*

As I started moving, Sadie whistled, drawing my attention upward. She winked at me and said, "Great speech."

I smirked.

People rehashed what had happened as the carts began to move again. Some spoke passionately about how close we'd come to death, while others feared that we might reencounter a similar situation.

I watched the forest as we moved, hopeful that the attack had been a one-time thing. I wasn't so sure we'd survive another.

As the sun began a slow descent, a cool breeze swept through the open field. I shivered and squeezed my spear closer against my chest.

"That doesn't look too good," came a man's voice.

It was the same old man from earlier—the one with a few strands of hair who had protected the medical cart. He aimed his large, crooked nose at the sky behind me.

Far away, the sky looked menacing.

Black clouds rolled and flashes of lightning lit up the sky. It wasn't near us, but it was close enough to cause concern. A few people turned their heads to watch the unfolding storm, and whispers broke out.

"We need to move faster," someone said.

"Maybe it won't come over here," came another voice.

Reina trotted toward us on her horse. "Let's speed things up a bit," she said, watching the distant clouds.

If Reina was worried, it meant Finn was worried, too, and that meant we were in danger.

Children pointed at the dark sky, asking their parents if it was dangerous. One mother stroked her son's dirty forehead, kissed him, and said, "Only if God lets it come near us."

This seemed to comfort the boy. He leaned his head against her chest and smiled, almost as if her very words had been enough to protect him. I, for one, wasn't willing to put my faith in the unseen. Reina was right—we needed to move faster.

"Switch!" Reina shouted, and people started jumping off the carts.

Those who were sore, or aching, climbed aboard, while those who had rested long enough started walking. The exchange was done as the carts were moving, with young adults helping the more vulnerable climb in and out.

Thunder roared nearby and I flinched.

The storm was moving closer. What would we do without shelter? Enter the forest? What about the animals? We couldn't possibly bring the carts inside—they wouldn't fit. Worse, we couldn't bring the sick and injured, either. Some of them were too weak to stand, let alone walk.

I searched the forest, the fields, and the vast open space up ahead. Could we make it to the bridge in time? The man in Finn's kitchen had spoken about there being a bridge that led to someplace called Port Williamson.

Would we find supplies there? What if people already lived there? Maybe we'd find shelter.

The unknown was enough to make my head spin, so I stopped worrying about the what-ifs and instead, concentrated on keeping a steady pace.

The only thing we could do right now was reach the bridge.

We walked quickly as the storm moved in, rumbling only a few miles away. Children shrieked when lightning came down—a bright flash of blue followed by an explosive cracking sound.

But it wasn't the thunder or the lightning that bothered me. It was the wind. It had started as a swift breeze, but now, it took my breath away. In the carts, people's hair danced in every direction as the wind hissed loudly.

With the sun now hiding behind the clouds,

everything was dark—almost as dark as nighttime. I'd seen dark clouds before but never like these—these were black. It was the strangest thing; at the opposite end of the sky, a line of orange ran horizontally, casting a yellow hue across the black clouds. It almost made them look brown. If we could only walk faster, maybe we'd outrun the storm.

"They're moving!" shouted a young girl.

Heads turned back to look at the approaching storm, and that was when I saw it—clouds moving in a circular motion. Around it, bright flashes of blue lit up the sky as the clouds swirled and spun, until finally, they took on a pointed shape.

Then, the monstrous swirl of clouds began to descend.

What was happening? Was this a *tornado*?

"Move, move, move!" Reina shouted.

She snapped her horse's reins and people panicked. The carts shook wildly as they picked up speed, and those on foot ran, trying to keep up. The wind became so loud that I couldn't hear what people were saying around me. Some pointed, their mouths opened wide, but I couldn't make out their words.

I ran along with the crowd, breathing out through tight lips to avoid losing my breath again. Every few seconds, I looked back, which felt like a mistake each time. The more the tornado took shape, the bleaker our survival seemed.

Its tip narrowed and spun as it slowly descended from the sky. Although the winds were moving at an impossible speed, the entire thing danced in slow motion. Its pointed tip finally made contact with the ground, creating a huge cloud of white. What was that? Dust? Debris?

We ran until my chest ached. Farther back, several people had stopped running. Some leaned forward, leaning the weight of their upper bodies onto their knees, while others looked like they were on the verge of collapsing. I wanted to help, but there were too many of them falling back.

Without warning, the carts stopped rolling and people slowed down.

What was going on? Why were we stopping? We couldn't stand here, waiting to be swept up by the tornado. Brushing past people, I made my way toward the front of the group.

Only then did I understand why we'd stopped moving.

I stared in disbelief, thinking my heart might climb into my throat.

People around me collapsed to their knees, some grabbing their hair, others holding on to their loved ones.

It was over.

We weren't surviving this.

Reina climbed off her horse and approached the river, where pieces of a bridge held on to the ledge. Across the river and up on land was the other side of the bridge, yet in the middle, only a few wooden planks remained.

We couldn't cross. All we could do was keep running, and by the looks of our people, it was unlikely we would outrun the storm.

"What now?" I shouted over the wind.

Reina looked at me, and for the first time, it became obvious she didn't know what to do. Like me, she probably believed this was over.

I felt guilty as my mind played out different scenarios: I could grab Sadie, and we could do our best to swim across the water. It wasn't that I wanted to leave people behind, but I didn't want to die. We had to try something, even if it meant not saving everyone.

When several young adults jumped into the river, I realized I wasn't the only one with this thought. The body of water was narrow here. Making it to the other side without getting caught in the current wasn't impossible. All it took was a bit of strength.

I was about to run to the medical cart when I felt a tickle under my feet. At first, it was subtle, like the feeling of Mother stomping through our house. But the vibrations became intense, tickling my calves and climbing up into my thighs.

Was this an *earthquake*? A few people froze with their arms outstretched on either side of them, looking as confused as I felt. A loud creaking sound joined the wind's threatening whistles, and farther up ahead, the ground began to split.

But this wasn't nature's doing.

The split was calculated—mechanical. As grass and earth fell from the rising door, an opening appeared, and out came a man holding a large black rifle.

I jumped back and gripped my spear.

Reina, too, prepared her bow, and one by one, Champions came forward, their weapons held high.

The door appeared to be made of metal and was easily the length of three carts side by side. It came up high, too. Even if the man had stretched his arm over his head, holding his gun, he wouldn't have been able to touch the top of it. Inside was a large cylinder-shaped tunnel that seemed to descend several miles underground. Although dim, it wasn't as dark as out here.

Little orange lights ran along the tunnel's ceiling, lighting the whole place up.

The man jabbed the tip of his gun at us and shouted something, but I couldn't make it out.

I stepped toward him, but Reina stuck an arm out, warning me to keep my distance.

The man shouted again.

What was he saying?

Ignoring Reina, I moved toward him.

"Put your weapons down!" he shouted.

I did as he demanded and laid my spear in the grass.

He jabbed his gun again. "Get inside!"

Who was this man? Was he dangerous, or was he trying to help us? He was an average-height man with medium-length brown hair, a salt-and-pepper beard, and a slender build. On his head was a brown, animal skin hat that covered the top of his hair. It was large and stuck out all around his head in a circular fashion. He wore beige pants and a white, bloodstained shirt. His brown boots matched his hat. When he regripped his gun, I noticed black stains all over his fingertips.

With his gun, he pointed at the approaching tornado and shouted, "Put your weapons down and get inside!"

Could it be he was trying to assist us?

I moved closer to him despite Reina shouting at me. As I came closer, cool air came out from inside the tunnel. It smelled fresh and crisp and reminded me a bit of the air in Olympus.

"Who are you?" I shouted.

"We really got time for that?" he shouted back. When a powerful wind blew between us, he grabbed his hat to keep it from flying off.

Behind me, Champions moved in with arrows and spears aimed at the man. He eyed them curiously, almost as if counting how many of us there were. Was he weighing his odds of winning the battle?

"Tell them to put down their weapons, or I revoke my offer," he said.

What offer was he referring to? Letting us inside? It was the only way to survive this storm. The only problem was, I didn't know this man. We didn't know this man. What if he turned out to be like the same people who had robbed us? What if once we entered, whoever lived here turned us into slaves? Abused us? Hurt us?

If we didn't go in, though, we would all die.

I inched even closer, and his gun turned on me. "Hands up!"

I stuck them up. I didn't want to fight. All I wanted was for everyone to survive the storm.

"How do we know we can trust you?" I shouted.

"You don't!" he said. It was obvious he was growing impatient as we watched the storm move closer and closer.

If we didn't act fast, he might turn around and close the door. "We can stand round here chitchattin' if that's what you want. Or, you can choose to live. You have ten seconds to decide."

I raised my hands even higher and stepped foot inside the metal opening.

He watched me curiously.

"We choose life," I said.

I turned to the people of Ortus, signaling them to follow.

"No weapons inside!" the man growled.

One by one, Champions lowered their weapons, their bows, spears, knives, and axes landing in the grass as everyone moved in. When the carts entered, their wheels made a loud clacking sound against the metal floor entrance.

"Come on, inside!" the man urged, waving a hand wildly.

By the time we all entered, the tornado was so close that weapons began floating into the air. The man reached for a button on the wall, smacked it, and stepped back as the heavy metal door above us came down.

The moment it closed, the storm's deafening howl stopped abruptly.

People bickered, some excited, others terrified.

"Who are you?" I asked the man.

"Don't worry about me," he said. "Let's get you people inside first, then we'll talk."

Although afraid to move forward—afraid we might meet bad people wanting to hurt us—I had to hope for the best. I had to believe that this man had helped us without any ill intentions.

"Thank you," I said to him.

He didn't smile, but he nodded, fixed his hat, and said, "Follow me."

He led me to the front of the group, then down the long concrete tunnel. It was so vast that people's voices and footsteps echoed everywhere.

I had so many questions, but I knew it was best to hold off for the time being. Right now, all that mattered was one thing—we were alive.

Wasn't that what counted?

Wasn't that why the Elites did what they did? Create a serum capable of granting immortality? To avoid death?

I breathed in the cool air, appreciating the feeling in my lungs.

Were we walking straight into danger? Maybe. But at least we were alive to face it together.

Visit **shadeowens.com** for more works by Shade Owens, including book #3 of The Immortal Ones series.

Made in the USA
Monee, IL
26 November 2022

18567959R00204